I0543317

MCCULLOUGH'S JAMBOREE BOOK 1

KATHI S. BARTON

This is a work of fiction. Names, characters, places, and incidents are products of the author's imagination or are used fictitiously and are not to be construed as real. Any resemblance to actual events, locations, organizations, or persons, living or dead, is entirely coincidental.

World Castle Publishing, LLC
Pensacola, Florida
Copyright © Kathi S. Barton 2016
Hardback ISBN: 9781629894324
Paperback ISBN: 9781629894331
eBook ISBN: 9781629894355
First Edition World Castle Publishing, LLC, February 22, 2016
http://www.worldcastlepublishing.com
Licensing Notes
All rights reserved. No part of this book may be used or reproduced in any manner whatsoever without written permission, except in the case of brief quotations embodied in articles and reviews.
Cover: Karen Fuller
Editor: Eric Johnston
Editor: Maxine Bringenberg

Prologue

Run. The single word screamed through her mind over and over while she lay hidden in her hiding place under the bed. They were at it again. Her parents never let the setting of the sun go by without hitting and screaming at one another, usually both. Sometimes her as well.

At twelve, RaeAnn just wanted to be safe. And even as young as she was, she knew other families weren't like hers. She wished every day that she'd not been born...at least not to these people.

The door to her room slammed back against the wall and startled a small whimper from her. Putting her hand over her mouth, she tried her best to not make another sound. Even breathing hard would bring her pain from them. The dark shadow could be either of them. Both her parents had a large build, long hair, and thick, mean hands.

"Girl!" her father screamed. "Come on out here. See to your mother so we can go to bed. You hear me? I said to get your skinny ass out here and fix her face up. It's bleeding from some kinda cut."

RaeAnn wouldn't help either of them by coming out of her hiding place. She'd learned her lesson the hard way about giving aid to one or both of them. Once she'd done what they wanted her to do, they'd find some little flaw with it and would knock her around until she was in worse shape than they had been. When the bed over her was suddenly gone, she held her breath harder, hoping that he'd not come any closer to her hiding place.

RaeAnn had skipped school over the course of several weeks to make this hiding space for herself, working until she was too exhausted to go on most days. Her parents were gone, no doubt to find somewhere that was giving something away, or digging through the dumpster to find a few thrown-away things that they could sell for a quick buck or two. They worked harder at that than they ever had at a job, she thought. But it was long enough for her to have gotten all the work done she needed without them knowing what she was about. Her hidey hole was perfect, so long as they didn't come too far into her room.

She'd taken up the floorboards. Most were rotted anyway and had been easy to remove. Then she'd dug out the dirt, just enough that she could use old bricks that had been stolen long ago to shore up the floor of the hole. Then she'd taken the dirt and filled old pop and beer cans to make up the rest of the walls around her when the bricks were gone. The place beneath her bed had less wind coming in than the room that she slept in, too.

"Girl, where the fuck are you?" He stomped into the room deeper, holding the dripping knife he had in his hand like he still meant business. Still she didn't move, even when a drop of whatever was wet on the knife dripped down on her cheek. RaeAnn knew that it was blood, his or her mother's, but she didn't move an inch to even wipe it from her. It was simply too dangerous right now.

He was standing on the last solid board before he got to the ones she'd had to makeshift to get her place ready; the first of many that she'd not removed to hide because it had been too solid for her to move without any tools, which she supposed was a good thing. One more, even half a step, and he'd be on top of her. His weight would crash upon her when he broke through to her.

Run, her mind screamed at her. *Run now!* But even if she did, there was no safe place for her to go. No neighbors that would offer her help, and certainly no one close enough that she could get to before one or both of her parents caught up with her again. Living in the middle of nowhere as they did, and using a long since abandoned house, there were little to no luxuries for her to use as a source of comfort.

No power and no heat. Water for some reason was plentiful, but it was ice cold even in the dead of summer, and even colder when there was snow on the ground, as there was now. Its source, as far as she could tell, was an underground well. A long hose from it to the house had given them at least some way to clean themselves…if her parents ever tried, that was.

They used lanterns for light mostly, but there was seldom money left over after beer and pop was bought to supply them with much more than a thimbleful of lantern oil. Candles, mostly birthday ones and some scented ones that would stink up the place rather than improve on the odors, would be what she'd do her homework by.

"Where is she?" Her mother stood in the doorway, her hulking frame blocking out the little moonlight that came in through the broken window in the living room. "She run off again?"

"Don't see her, do you? Fucking moron. What the fuck is wrong with you? Ain't you done heard me calling out for her to come and help you out? She's not in here now, is she?" Her mom called her father an asshole and they were at it again. This time in her room.

As they tumbled out, their fists hitting whatever was close enough to them, she heard them grunting in pain. Nothing was safe. RaeAnn cried silently as they continued to fight. Nothing in her room was worth worrying about, nor was there anything that she treasured.

It wasn't long before the silence became enough that she knew they'd either killed each other, which she prayed would happen nightly, or they'd finally tired themselves out. RaeAnn didn't move. She wasn't stupid enough to think that the coast was clear just yet. Another ploy that she'd been caught in. She would wait them out, even if it took all night.

RaeAnn must have dozed off at some point. Her room was deadly silent, the place bright with the sun. There wasn't any sound coming from the rest of the house, so she moved her body first, trying to work out the sore places before she stood up. If she had to run, she wanted to be as ready as she could be.

They were gone. She could see that now. Lifting herself out of the hole, she could see beyond to the other room. The shack was only the three rooms, not even a bathroom inside the place other than a commode that rarely worked and the hose that was brought in from the well in a curtained off area in the living room to wash-up with when it was necessary. RaeAnn did a wash up every day, but she knew that her parents did only when it was too much for them to sleep together. Moving out of the house, she kept an eye out for them.

She had no coat or shoes that she could put on despite the cold weather. They were both somewhere in the house, she knew that. But she could only use them when she was going to school, and had to remove them both and turn them in every day to whoever was there when she got home. It was like the library, she thought...only on loan to her until she could no longer wear them. Which was pretty much where she was with both pieces of clothing now.

Not bothering to grab up anything, RaeAnn made her way out of the house and took off at a run toward the woods. She had no idea what was this way. The bus picked her up about a mile from the house in the opposite direction, but she figured that this was her best bet at getting away. This time, RaeAnn thought, she was staying away from them.

Her feet were hurting when she'd gone no more than an hour from the house. But she didn't stop. Stopping now would get her caught, so she kept her eye on the mountain in front of her — her guiding light, so to speak — and kept going. She'd make it or die, which was a good possibility right now. RaeAnn was cold and starving, but she was freer now than she'd ever been.

It had been dark for some time when she came upon the barn. Cows and a bull had been in a field that she'd gone around, and she'd kept an eye on the massive bull that seemed to move along with her but yet never came at her. When the barn's light went off, RaeAnn stood by the tree she was nearest as a few deer moved, then the light flickered on again. As she watched, the light went off and on twice more before the deer moved on, and she knew they were the cause of it.

Slipping into the barn had been easy. It was a good deal warmer than it was outside, and the snow had just begun to fall again. Several inches blanketed the ground already, and RaeAnn knew that she was making the perfect path for her parents to find her. But right now, she was too hungry and hurting too badly to care if they found her or not. She moved to the bales of hay and lay down on the parts that were broken off. RaeAnn knew that she should keep moving, but decided that she could do so better if she had a little nap.

~~~

Peter kissed his lovely wife on the cheek as he made his way out to the barn. They had a lot of things to do today, and one of them was to put together the new baby bed that had arrived just yesterday. In three months they'd be parents, and he was as tickled about that as he could be.

As soon as he opened the barn door, he knew something was wrong. A girl was standing at the feed bin to one of his prized cows, talking. And she was eating the feed and telling the poor cow staring at her that she was so sorry, but her belly was too empty for her to not take what she could. Peter cleared his throat as gently as he could, and fell back when she came at him with a pitchfork. As it was, he was pinned tightly against the barn wall as she stared at him with more fear than he had.

"I'm not gonna hurt you." Nothing, just that...it took him a few seconds to realize that she was fevered. "You need me to call someone for you? I can. My wife is just in the house and I can have her call your parents for —"

"I won't go back." He nodded, not sure what she meant, but right now he'd agree with her if she told him he was a woman. "I won't go back. Please don't make me."

"All right." He reached for his wife and told her what was going on. He also told her to bring her medical bag. He thought the girl was sick and his wife might be able to help her before he called the police. "My wife is coming out now. She's a doctor and can help you."

"I don't want to go back there. Don't make me, please." The door opened and he didn't look to see if it was his wife or not. The girl still had the fork at his chest, and he knew that if something startled her, he'd never see his child being born. "I won't go back."

"I won't make you. You just have to let me go now." He looked her over, trying to see if there were any other weapons on her that he needed to know about, and saw the blood on her bare feet. "Where are your shoes? And coat?"

"It's not a school day." He had no idea what she meant by that, but she continued before he could ask. "I can't have them unless it's a school day. Please don't make me go back."

"Put that down right now." Peter closed his eyes when Mary spoke harshly to the girl. "What do you think you're doing? I said put it down."

The glazed look turned from him to look at his wife. Peter wanted to knock the fork away, but he knew that being stupid right now would get them both killed. The girl's hand started to tremble and the fork came closer to his chest.

"I don't want to go back." Mary told the girl that she wasn't going anywhere, that she needed to put the fork down. The girl looked at it like she only just realized that she had it, and it lowered to the floor. "I can just go now. I can just leave and you don't have to worry about me coming back. I'm not going back there again."

"Come on now, you just sit right down and let me have a look at those cuts." Mary spoke softly now as she took the fork from the girl completely and handed it to him. "Peter, go on up to the house and run a bath...well, make that a shower. And find me something that I can soak her poor feet in."

Nodding, he didn't want to leave his very pregnant wife with this child, but she seemed to have things under control at the moment. There was something very off about the girl and it frightened him, not just a little. But Mary told him she was just fine and for him to put the kettle on too.

"I don't think we have time for tea, Mary. This girl tried to kill me." Mary only patted him on the cheek and told him to go on now. He was in the house filling the kettle before he realized she'd out moved him. Again.

Ever since he'd met her, thinking her well out of his league, she'd been out moving him. He'd say something and she'd sort of agree with him, but he'd end up doing it her way anyway. Usually she was right...well, she was always right. Like them buying this farm and raising cattle. Some of them big things, others not so much, but she'd bring him around to her way of thinking before he knew what hit him. She was good at that.

When he went back out to the barn, the girl was asleep. Mary told him she'd given her something for pain, and her exhaustion and starvation had taken her under. He looked at the girl now and could see that wherever she'd come from, it had been a long hard way.

"I don't think she's eaten a proper meal in a good long time, if ever. And she kept telling me that she'd not go back. I was wondering if you'd do me a favor." He knew what she wanted and he wasn't going to do it. "We have to know if they're in worse shape than she is. What if someone came to wherever it is she was living and killed her whole family, and she got away?"

"That's pretty farfetched, even for you." She did that smile thing again, the thing that made him fall in love with her the moment he'd first seen her. Even before he realized she was his mate. "You want me to go and find where she's been and see if her family is dead. They could be the ones that were abusing the poor thing; you know that, right?"

"I do." He started peeling off his shirt. "When you get back, I'll have you a thick stack of pancakes and some bacon all ready for you. And if you run into trouble, you can call me and I'll come and rescue you."

"I don't care for you much right now." She laughed, and he bent to pick up the girl when Mary started to. "I'll take her in the house, but I want you to stay away from her until I get back. Promise?"

"I'll try to keep away from her." As they made their way into the house, his burden, he just realized, was lighter than most of the animals they had on the property. Peter decided that he didn't mind so much that Mary was smarter than him. He loved her that much. He asked Mary how the girl had fared this long. "She's been starved, Peter. And I don't think this is a recent thing. Look at her feet and hands. She's been running for a long distance for some reason, and it frightens me to think she was out there all night without anything to keep her warm or fed."

"I'll go and see what I can find." He laid the girl on the bed and then looked at Mary. "Don't let her hurt you, love. You're all I have in the world."

"We'll be fine, I promise."

Peter let his cat take him. His jaguar was glad for the change and stretched twice as he made his way to the kitchen to leave. Again he told Mary to be careful, and she promised him she would. Peter had the girl's scent, but he only had to follow the footpaths in the snow to find where she'd come from. The blood mixed with the wet falling snow was like a calling card for his cat.

He'd gone perhaps five or six miles when he came upon the building. He was sure that the girl had come from there. Her scent had let him right to it. But to call it a home…Peter was sure that his falling down shed at home had fewer holes in the roof, and the wood would hold out a bit more of the cold too.

Peter didn't get any closer to it than ten feet because there were humans inside, but he knew that he had to eventually. The scent was fresh blood, and he needed to be assured that no one else inside was hurt. He was sure, as sure as anything he'd ever felt, that the girl at his house had spent if not her whole life there, then the biggest part of it. His heart broke for her.

The loud voices were violent in nature, and he knew that the sounds coming from the house were people fighting, not just verbally but physically as well. As he made his way closer to the house, he kept an eye out for anyone coming out of the falling down building. Peter didn't want to get in the middle of anything that was going on right now.

The child had come from this house; he knew it when he crossed over the broken steps onto the porch. There was no doubt about it. And the scents also told him that the people living there had had contact with her. They were related, the three of them, and he was pretty sure that the girl was running from them. As they fell out of the house and into the yard, still hitting each other, Peter made his way into the house through the broken door at the back of the wrap-around porch that had seen better days.

Peter nearly left again, thinking that this could not be a place where people were living, a home. Or what was left of one. But he made his way around the bigger room and found that the girl had been in there a great deal. Then he made his way to one of the other rooms that shot off from the larger one in the middle.

It was hers. He knew that from how strong he could smell her. The bed was broken and shattered against the wall and the floorboards had been ripped up at some point, and he knew that was where she'd hidden before leaving. Peter looked around the room and could see that while it was dirty, it was better kept than the room he'd just left.

There were no pictures on the walls, no girly things to indicate that a child lived there. The bed had a threadbare blanket on it, and no pillow to speak of. The mattress was thinner than his overcoat that he wore in the fall, and the neat stack of clothing in the corner was small and pitiful even for a child. Not even a dresser to put things on, much less inside of it. He moved to the deep hole and looked inside.

Haven. That was all he could think of when he saw what she'd done. Because to Peter, there was little doubt that she'd done this to keep herself safe. Looking around again, he tried to imagine living there. Hearing those people still screaming at each other in the yard, he could not fathom how a person could stand this every day of their life. Moving back through the bedroom, he looked into what he thought was used as a living room.

A couch that was held up on one end with a cinder block sagged dangerously in the middle. The person who chanced sitting there would spill out onto the floor if they weren't careful as to how they sat. No television graced the walls, and that was when he realized there was no hum of power in the house. The heat, too, was off, if there had ever been any, and he was chilled when an errant breeze blew through the open door.

A curtain was hanging across an area in front of him. Moving slowly toward it, testing the floors as he went, Peter was almost afraid to see what was there; the bathroom, or a makeshift one. A commode sat over a too large hole in the floor, with no plumbing to speak of, and that thought made his belly slightly ill. A hose hung from a hole in the wall with a dirty towel next to it. The dripping water was freezing in a long stream beneath it, and looked as lethal as any knife or tool he had at his home.

Backing out of the room with the toilet and to his right, he moved through the curtain into another bedroom. A mattress on the floor looked as flat as a board, and probably no more comfortable. Several pillows of varying thickness, from paper thin to almost an inch thick, were at the head of it. Against the walls, all the way around, were piles of junk.

Broken games, torn books, heaters that had been torn apart—for parts, he assumed—and tossed aside instead of dealt with were in the trash. Newspapers that were yellowed with age. Boxes of dented canned goods that he knew were bad even from where he stood. Open bags of chips and popcorn were spread everywhere. Candy bar wrappers and junk food galore littered nearly every available surface of the nasty floor, along with dirty stacks of clothing, stiff with dirt and filth.

Cardboard, like in the other two rooms, covered the windows. There was a little plastic on one of them, but it had long since broken free of the push pins that held it there. It flapped in the wind much like the pretty flag that his wife had in the yard that had their last name on it. Burcher.

Peter? I can feel that you're upset. What did you find? He didn't want her to know, but knew also that keeping it from her would eat him alive. He told her what he'd found and who the people were the girl was hiding from. *Oh, that poor little thing. To live like that. What do you think we should do?*

Peter wanted to tell her that he was going to kill them both, tear their throats out and leave them for the rats and buzzards to fill their bellies on. The feeling was something that he'd never had before, not in all his twenty-seven years. But he also knew that he'd regret it, even if he felt good about it now.

Don't call the police. Don't tell anyone that she's there. And if she wakes and tells you that she's not going back, you assure her that she isn't. Not so long as I'm alive she won't. He heard the couple on the lawn again and moved to the window to get a good look at them. *These people deserve to die out here. Where no one will know who they are. And they don't deserve to have that little girl. People like them should be...Mary, I want to kill them both where they are.*

Come home to us. He said he was on his way and looked at the kerosene heater that burned in the living room. The heat, what little the heater was giving off, was being whisked away by the cold that blew through the house like it wasn't even there. He moved the pillow that had fallen to the floor just a little closer to it. To his way of thinking, if they found it, great; if not, what were they out? Nothing as far as he could see. As he left the house, he decided that he hoped they didn't find it. He thought they should suffer as much as the child had that was in his home.

"Where is that fucking girl? RaeAnn, damn you girl, when I find you, you're going to hurt for a damned month this time." Peter paused to listen to the man yelling again. "RaeAnn Richards, I'm going to beat your ass again. See if I don't."

You won't, Peter thought as he moved out of the broken window. The flame started to flare up just as he heard the man outside stomping his way up and onto the porch before hearing the jingle of keys somewhere. Hiding deep in the trees, Peter watched the man make his way to a part of the yard he'd not noticed to the big car that had been covered with dead branches and trees. As soon as the engine roared to life, Peter knew that by the time they returned, the house or whatever it was would be gone, and so would all traces of the girl he and Mary were going to raise as their own.

Peter made his way back to his house. He was feeling better about what he'd done to the house with every step he took. It wasn't fit to live in, he thought, and now that it was gone, perhaps the people there would move away and forget they had a little girl. Although he was pretty sure they'd done that already. After shifting to his human side and dressing, Peter kissed his wife and told her what he'd done.

"Good." He cocked a brow at her, thinking that she'd be at least a little upset with him over it. "Damned people. They should be horsewhipped."

His wife never cursed, and to hear her to do so now made him realize that something more had happened. He asked her about it and she burst into tears. Taking her to the bedroom where RaeAnn still slept, he watched in horror as she pulled back the blanket that laid over her and showed him what she'd discovered.

"They branded her. Who does something like that? They put a hot iron to her skin and burned it. Just like she was one of our cows." He ran his finger over the newly burned skin and felt his heart break. "There are scars on her back too. Like they'd beaten her with a whip. And her feet, they're going to take a long time to heal. The poor thing. I don't want to let her go, Peter. We have to keep her here and safe."

"We are. We will." He heard the sirens screaming by the farm and smiled. He knew it would be a total loss, and he was even more glad he'd done it now. "Her name is RaeAnn Richards. When she wakes up and is feeling better, I'll have someone fix up the paperwork with her a new name and identity on it."

"Good. She'll be a Burcher and we'll love her as our own." Peter hoped it would be that way, but for all they knew the girl was just as bad as her parents. Then he thought of the hole she'd made.

"She'll be a good girl. And we'll make sure she has what she needs too." Yes, Peter thought as he held Mary, she'd be a good addition to their family. Now he had to figure out how to tell her that her new parents were jaguars.

KATHI S. BARTON

Chapter 1

"I don't know." If Colin heard that one more time, he was going to tear the man's heart out. "You think maybe it's because they don't know what it's used for?"

"You think maybe they can't read?" Colin looked at the man standing in front of him then looked at the wall where the instructions were plainly printed and wondered what the fuck he was doing there. Oh yeah, he was watching over a failing plant for the man that had been a family friend for decades. And his dad had asked him to see what was going on. "I want you to find out why someone would sabotage a perfectly good lift for no other reason than they could."

"How do you suppose they got it to tilt like that? You think they had to bring them in another one to do that?"

Colin just growled and walked away. He was done talking to the idiot for now. Maybe even for good.

He'd asked the man several questions. Who did this? I don't know. How long ago had this happened? I don't know. Are there cameras here? I don't know. Colin was ready to shift and tear the man apart. But he also knew that it would do him little to no good; the man still wouldn't have the answers he needed.

The forklift—or just lift, as he'd figured out they had called the piece of machinery since his family had come in to help this company several weeks ago—was leaning nearly level with the floor as it rested on a wooden box. The only way that he could think that someone would have been able to do that to it was to have a second lift there to bring it over, and then a third one to lower it to the ground enough that it rested on the wooden crate it was currently on. He had no idea why everyone thought it was funny, but now he was going to have to go over footage of the plant to see who the fuck had just gotten themselves fired. Then call in a crew to set it upright and make sure that no damage had been done to it.

When his phone rang, he jerked it out of his pocket, tearing the seam there, and nearly threw the cursed thing across the floor. Barking his name into the device, he knew the moment he did it that he should have checked to see who was calling him, and maybe he might have lived another day.

"I see. And this is why you're in charge? You have the meanest, loudest voice? Or is it your lovely temperament? I'm sure that has a great deal to do with it, don't you?" He started to tell his mom he was sorry, but she was on a roll now. "Or could it be that you're Colin McCullough and everyone needs to bow down before you or feel your wrath? Is that it? Because, son, I'm not at all impressed with you at the moment."

"I'm not having a good day." She tisked at him. "There are people here that I'm going to have to fire because they think that taking a twenty-thousand dollar piece of equipment and turning it into a play thing is funny. Not to mention there is so much that needs to be repaired anyway, that I'm not sure how this place has remained in business for as long as it has. It's a mess here."

The loud crash behind him didn't even make him turn. It had been only a matter of time before the empty shipping crate broke under the weight of the lift and fell to the floor. He moved into his office with extreme care not to slam the door, because he knew his mom could hear it.

"I was hoping you'd be able to come over for dinner tomorrow night. Your dad and I miss you." He missed them as well. It had been a couple of weeks since he'd been able to leave, and he needed family like he needed air to breathe. "Hawkins is coming home in a few days too. He's only going to be here for a little over a week before he ships out again, and I thought it would be nice to have the entire family together at least once or twice."

Hawkins had been gone for a long time this time, nearly two years. He was in the service and had been overseas more than home in the last few years. His brother was going to make a career of the army, he'd told Colin when he'd been home last, and he was happy to know he'd found a home of sorts for himself.

"What time? And I'm not making any promises, but I'll do my best." He knew that he'd be there even if he had to close down the plant for a day to make it. "And what can I bring? I'm sure I can find a deli open somewhere that has sandwiches that I can bring."

His mom did not cook. She could turn on the stove if pressed and could sometimes make popcorn in the microwave if she was paying attention, but cooking was something she'd never been good at. She used to tell them that if they wanted a hot meal for breakfast before the cook came in, there was the microwave to heat up their cereal.

But his mom loved with all that she was, and that to him was more than enough.

"Your father is laughing too hard to answer me just now, and so you know, I might beat your bottom when you get here. His too while I'm at it." Colin felt the stress of the day roll off him. That was what he needed. Family. "I need to speak to you about a few things here as well. Your father and I are making out our will and we need to get some things settled."

"No." She asked him what. "Please. Not today. Or when I come home. I'm not ready for that just yet. It's just too soon. I know that it has to be done, but not just after Great-Grandda died. Okay?"

She was so quiet that he knew that she was feeling the pain of it too. Her grandda had been a solid figure in all their lives since forever. Colin had been named for him. They had been close, and he'd been a spry happy man right up until he'd gone to bed one night and had simply not woken up. He'd been ninety-five years old.

"All right. But we must talk about it sooner rather than later. I don't want the...you know what a mess he left for me." He did too. The family lawyer was still trying to sort out what was what. "Just...soon, all right? I don't want to leave this for you boys to deal with."

After he hung up with her, making plans to have his house opened up for him, Colin thought of his brothers. None of them, he knew, would want to think about their parents needing a will, much less leaving them. All six of them, including him, needed their parents much like a babe did their mother's breast.

Colin was the oldest, and he supposed that was why his mom wanted to talk to him. He had no idea why she cared about that sort of thing. All of them were level-headed enough to talk about death and wills. But it was a pecking order, she'd told him once. And he was the oldest rooster she could peck.

Hawkins was next at nearly two years younger than him. He had joined the service just out of high school and had now served nearly seventeen years, most of which had been working to end one conflict after another. But he liked it and seemed to enjoy the rigidness of the daily routine.

Boyd was a doctor in his own practice now. He'd done his time working in larger companies, being one of many that would see patients in a hurry-up-and-get-them-out way. He'd hated it, and at one point had decided to go back to college to become something else. But Great-Grandda had told him to quit, find a building, and remodel it. The two of them had spent nearly a year working on it daily, turning an old grade school into a large daycare center, which he sold and bought another building to work on as he became a doctor he could like again. His practice was booming.

Parker was a farmer. Not just raising crops, but also horses, something that he'd never thought a shifter would have been able to keep. But he'd worked with younger ponies and raised them up to not only not be afraid of him and his kind, but other shifters as well. He had several other kinds of paranormals working with him, and they all helped to make them compatible with their kind.

Larson worked with Colin. When their great-grandda had been alive, he'd opened an investment bank of sorts for paranormals. Back then it had been harder for shifters to get loans to get their businesses up and running, so his great-grandda had decided that he had some money to spare and would help out. Regular banks would take one look at the fact that people who wanted to borrow money were a member of a certain group, namely non-humans, and they would be turned down. The family business had made them very wealthy and well respected.

Colin and Larson had started helping those same businesses when it looked as if they were going to go under. Even some of them that didn't owe them any more money would ask for help, and he and Larson would gladly assist. Up until recently, it had been a lot of fun to see things work out. Now he simply missed having his great-grandda there to talk to.

Dustin was the baby of the family at twenty-seven, and was still trying to find his way. Not that he didn't have a college degree—he'd been working toward becoming a lawyer in his own practice—but lately, unlike the rest of them, he'd found that he wasn't cut out for a certain type of office job.

But Dustin had been working with their dad on revamping houses, buying cheap and selling for a lot more. It worked for them, kept them both out of Mom's hair, she said, but Colin worried for his baby brother in that he still lived at home and didn't go out much. Maybe he'd work on that when he got there.

Not that he dated all that much either. At thirty-seven, the appeal of going out every night of the week had finally run its course. He loved women, everything about them. But most of the time he felt bored with them. They did what he wanted, said what they thought he wanted to hear, and seemed to be more interested in their cell phones and taking pictures of anything and everything, so that he'd end up taking them home early and not dating again for a couple of weeks. While he thought the cell phone was very useful, it was also a pain in the ass. His rang just as he was getting up to see if he could find some surveillance tape on the forklift incident.

"Mr. McCullough, Colin McCullough?" The voice was hard and full of something that scared him a little. He told the caller that was who he was. "This is Major General Anthony Phillips. I'm calling about your brother, Hawkins McCullough. He's been...there's been a shooting and men are down, and—"

"Is he alive?" No answer. Colin grabbed the side of his desk and asked again. "Tell me, damn it. I want to know if my brother is dead."

"Yes. He's alive. Christ." The man sounded like he was crying, and Colin slid to the floor. If something could make a man that sounded like he'd been around awhile and might have seen it all cry, Colin wasn't sure he wanted to hear it. "His squad is...nineteen of them and only three survivors. Your brother and his CO are being airlifted out now. The last man...we're not sure he's going to make it. They walked into some major shit and it went south fast. We're still working out the details, but so far all we can tell for certain is that there are a lot of dead men here."

Colin asked where they were. And after he was told, Colin sat at his desk again and started a search. "My brother was coming home in a couple of days. How the hell did this happen? And you've not called my parents, have you? Please tell me that you didn't. I'm not there yet and I don't want them to hear this right now when they're alone."

"No. No, we have...I was given instructions by all the men on who to call and not to call. McCullough's file says you and only you. I have a few orders like that. A couple of them said they'd hunt me down if I called their mommies. One man said that if I called his mom, he'd sic her on me.

Scary thought that...I met her." The man was babbling, and Colin didn't blame him. Sixteen dead men. He'd be making a lot of very emotional calls over the next few hours. "I'm making one more call to a family before I...I'm also making arrangements to have family meet up at the hospital that they're being flown to. When I have the—"

"I have a plane. I'll make my own arrangements. Just tell me where to go and when." Phillips said thanks but nothing else. Colin wondered what had happened to Hawkins and how bad it was when the man started talking again.

"Your brother...he's a good man. And from what I've been able to gather, he saved his CO and the other man by pulling them to safety. I don't know what was going on. Honestly I don't, but I do know that I'll get to the bottom of this. Your brother, he's in a bad way, but I think...what he is, it's going to help him where it didn't the others. I lost a good...they were good men, all of them, but this thing...this thing should never have happened."

"I understand."

After Phillips told Colin where he could meet them, he hung up. Now he had to make the hardest call of his life. He had to call his mom and dad. Picking up the phone again, he called the plant manager and told him he was leaving.

"Leaving? You can't do that. I have you here for a week yet." Colin told him that there had been an accident and he had to go. "I'm sorry about that, but you said you'd help me out. I can't let you go. Whatever it is, you'll have to have someone else deal with it. I'm not ready for you to go yet. I'm still losing money here daily, and I'm not letting you go."

"Well, I guess it really sucks to be you. I'm leaving right now and there is little to nothing you can do about it. Not that I think you can, but I'm out of here." Colin was out the door when he saw the man coming out of his office. To be honest, Colin didn't think there was any saving the company, and just knowing that the man was there and not out on the floor with him trying to figure out the business sealed the deal. "You'll be hearing from my firm in a few days, Mr. Mason. Have a good day."

Leaving wasn't as hard as he'd thought it would be. As soon as he was in his car to leave, he put in his ear piece and dialed his dad. Not that he didn't think his mom could handle the news, but he knew that his dad could work the phone so they could both hear him better than she could. That was another thing his mom hadn't been able to work well, computers or anything that worked like them. As soon as his dad answered, Colin felt the weight of the world on his shoulders.

~~~

Peter returned the phone to the cradle. Then he sat down hard, the floor beneath him unforgiving. Looking up at his son's face, he tried to focus on what he was saying, but all he could hear was the ringing in his head, loud and persistent. When he felt his head snap around, he looked into the face of his mate. She had smacked him, and he hurt for them both all over again.

"Lauren has been hurt, badly." Mary joined him on the floor. "I don't know much other than she's still alive but in bad shape. Her boss just told me he's sending a car for us to get on a plane to go to her."

"When?" He told her within the hour. "All right. We have to get ready to go then. I'll pack. You call someone in to take care of the farm for us. Call Patrick. His sons are home."

Nodding, he stood up on wobbly knees and made the call. Just having talked to Mary for those few seconds gave him strength. And a purpose. His Mary was always good at that. His son Pete was sitting at the table when he got off the phone with Patrick, who said it would be no problem to keep an eye on his herd and the buildings.

"She gonna die?" He told his son that he didn't know. "I'm going as well. I...she's my sister, and I'm going as well."

"Of course you are. She'd want you there too." He had no idea. All he could think about was that Lauren was hurt, and it tore badly at him that once again he'd not been there to protect her. She was...the lost little girl that had come into their life was hurt again. "We need to pack up. Go see to your things for me."

As soon as Pete left him, Peter sat in the chair he'd just left. Lauren, his daughter. She was his world and not even of his blood. He thought of the first time he'd spoken to her about being a part of his family twenty years ago, he just realized.

"I'm not human." Her nod had him thinking that she didn't get it. "I'm a shifter, a jaguar. My wife is as well, and our child will be too."

"Will you make me go back to them? I'll do anything you need for me to — clean, cook, take care of everything — if you don't make me go back there." He told her that the house had burnt to the ground while she'd been sleeping the three days she'd been out. "So they're coming here too then?"

"No. Not ever. Mary and I have talked and we'd like for you to stay with us. Be our child. We'd like for you to stay here and be our child." RaeAnn, her name had been then, didn't answer him. "We'll have to make some changes. Your name for one thing. And we'll make sure that no one knows who you are to them either."

"All right." He said nothing but watched her face. He'd never seen someone with such a sad and lonely face before. "You won't make me go back? I promise you, you'll never have to worry about me being bad. I promise you, I'll be the best person you ever met."

"I know that."

And she had been too. When Pete was born, she'd helped Mary out around the house and cared for Pete any time they needed her to. When he was older and going to school, she spent countless hours working with him on his homework, keeping him in line, and making sure he knew the value of an education. Even with the age difference between them, they were close and had continued to be close when she'd left for the service at eighteen. Unless people asked or knew that she was human, everyone assumed that Lauren was their daughter and Pete's older sister. Peter couldn't have asked for better kids than the two he had right now.

The limo arrived an hour later. After they were loaded into it and on their way, his cell phone rang again. It was the major general again. Peter closed his eyes, thinking this was the call he'd dreaded since he'd called him a bit ago.

"The car will take you and your family to the airport, and from there, you'll be taken to the hospital landing strip. It's a military zone, so if you're armed, I'm afraid that you'll have to leave your weapons behind." He told him that none of them carried even a knife. "Good. Once you are in the hospital there will be military personnel everywhere. Ask for me. I'm here now waiting on the life flight to land. Their

ETA is about ten minutes. Once they are here, both Burcher and her soldier will be taken directly to surgery. I'm sorry, but there won't be any time for you to see your daughter before she goes in."

"How is she?" He told him that he'd not had any communications with the chopper since it left the site. "But you have to know something. Anything."

"I'm sorry. All I know is that she and this other soldier are on their way in, and that it's bad for them both." He asked about the last man. "He passed. His wounds were...they were great, and he was only human as well. But Lauren and one of her men are on their way in now."

"As is my daughter—human, I mean." There was no response to that, and Peter reached for Mary's hand. "You'd tell me, wouldn't you, if she didn't make it in? Right?"

"I can only tell you what I know, Mr. Burcher. And the last contact that I had with the medics told me that she was in critical condition, and that they didn't expect her to make it this far." There was silence at the other end, but Peter heard a door close and the noises in the background simply stop. "Lauren is the best man I have ever met. Strong tempered, loyal to a fault, and stubborn as hell. If anyone can make it, human or otherwise, it will be her. I don't want to lose her any more than you do. She's...we fight a great deal, argue over everything, but she's the best at what she is. They were...what I'm telling you now is classified. What they walked in on, what happened to them...all I can tell you is that as soon as I find out what the fuck happened, I will promise you heads will roll and I will make them pay for this."

"What was she doing? What job...she couldn't tell us anything. Not even where she was. Is that what this is about? Her being somewhere that she shouldn't have been?" He told him that it wasn't something he could share with him. "My daughter is dying and you can't share with me? I shared her with you, you motherfucking asshole. You damned well had better tell me something."

"She was on a mission that should have been cut and dried. Not easy, never that if they're called in, but nothing like this should have happened. They were ambushed. Whoever did this, they knew that they were coming in, how they were coming in, and when." Peter said nothing. He wasn't sure what to say. They'd been betrayed. "They walked into a situation that should have been cut and dried, but it meant all their deaths. Or nearly so. All those men, all of them are dead but your daughter and one other man. And those two that escaped, I have a feeling that this won't end here. Whoever did this, they wanted her entire squad dead."

Peter didn't have anything to say and closed the connection. Someone wanted his daughter dead. There was someone out there, right now, upset...pissed that she had lived. Who? Why? What had she been doing that would...? He looked over at his wife and held her as she quietly cried. Pete, sitting across from him, wiped at tears as well. Peter didn't know what he'd do if he lost her. He didn't know what any of them would do without her in their lives.

As soon as they were at the airstrip, their luggage was unloaded as they were helped onto a large plane. He wasn't sure what sort of plane it was, didn't care either, but he knew that this was not the sort of service that people would normally receive when a loved one was hurt. As they were set up on the large private belly of the plane, a woman in a uniform came to ask them if they needed anything. When they declined, she handed them each a badge, complete with their picture on it, as well as a thick file.

"This is where you will be staying. The hotel has arranged service to take you to and from the hospital each day. Food will be brought to you, as will any other things you need when you are not at the hotel." Pete asked about Lauren. "I'm sorry, sir. I'm not privy to that information. I am a liaison for the army to help personnel in these sort of situations. The president will be calling you this evening. When he does, you are not to tell anyone of your conversation with him, nor do you talk to the press about anything you might see or hear. Understood?"

"The president of what?" The woman, Agent Carols, told him. "The president of the United States is going to call me? Why?"

"He is your daughter's boss, and he is most upset about what has happened to her and her men." Peter looked at his wife, then back at the agent. "When he calls you, please keep in mind it will be a private call between you and your family. Please do not share anything he might say to you."

"We won't."

As she continued with the rules and regulations as to what they should expect when they landed, all Peter could think about was that his daughter knew the president, and that he was upset that she'd been hurt. He wondered how that had happened. And why.

Chapter 2

Lauren woke but didn't move. She had no idea where she was or what the fuck had happened. One minute she'd been trying her damnedest to get out of a building that was supposed to be unoccupied, and the next she hurt everywhere. Ordering her men out...she did remember that, and that...blood, there was a lot of blood. Turning her head slowly, not sure still what had happened to her physically, she could see her dad sitting asleep in the chair and Pete looking out the window. He turned and looked at her, and she wondered what he was doing there too.

"Mom went to get some tea. Dad hasn't been sleeping well since we got here." She said nothing at his whispered explanation. "We've been here about two weeks now. I thought you were going to sleep right through it all. And so you know, you look like crap. Warmed over crap, as a matter of fact."

"Hurt." He nodded and moved closer to her. Everything was blurry, and when he got closer, she noticed how tall he'd gotten. "Tall. Grown up."

"Yeah, that happens when you leave home for years and years. People around you have to grow up and take your place." He pulled her hand to his mouth and kissed it. "Do you have any idea how terrified we were when they called us? How no one is telling us anything that happened to you?"

"Sorry, it's classified." Closing her eyes, she let the pain wash over her. It was good, the pain; it meant she could feel and that she wasn't dead. "Where am I?"

"A military hospital right outside of New York. If they told us the name, I don't remember it." She did and looked at him again. "We're supposed to tell them if you wake up. They don't want us to talk to you about anything. I guess you have to be debriefed or something like that."

She supposed she would be. It had been…everything about that fated trip had been wrong. So wrong that she'd been on the radio trying to get answers even as the place was blowing up around them. And her men were being shot to shit and dying.

"Don't leave." He said that he wasn't going anywhere. "My men, do you know anything? Did any of them make it out?"

"No. Nothing. There is one guy here with you, but I don't know a lot about him either. They're keeping everything hush hush." She could see that. The army was nothing but one big secret. "Do you hurt? Bad?"

"Yes. Everything." He didn't say anything, and she looked at him. He was crying and trying his best not to. "I'm not going to die. I'm too stubborn for that."

"That's what that guy told Dad when we got here. He said if someone told you that you were not going to make it, you'd live just to be right. He said that you were ten kinds of stubborn." She knew who it was without being told: Tony Phillips. "He's one scary-assed dude. He said you were scarier."

"I am. Don't forget it either." The pain was making itself known to her, and she asked Pete what he knew about her injuries. But before he could answer her, she saw her dad standing over her. "Hi there, Dad. You think they'll let me go home with you now?"

He started crying, heart wrenching sobs that hit her right in the heart. He kept telling her how much he loved her, needed her in his life, and she could only let him hold her hand while her own battle with tears was falling apart.

Most of her men and those that commanded her would have said that Lauren Burcher didn't have any feelings, but they'd be wrong. Her family was her life. Peter and Mary Burcher had taken her in and made her a part of something she'd never had before. Love. And family. Then they'd done one more for her: they'd given her a little brother. Pete Burcher was the best thing in the world to her.

Pete left them after a few minutes. He said that he was going to find Mom, and Dad sat in his chair, never letting go of her hand. Dad told her what he knew, which was very little, and that he loved her. And told her over and over again that he was glad to see her awake and that he wasn't leaving her.

"What happened to me? I know that I'm pretty beat up, but how bad is it?" He looked around the room, then back at her. "Dad?"

"They said we weren't to tell you anything. Not until they talked to you. Something about you having to tell them what you knew so they could let you share only what they wanted you to. Sounds like a cover up to me." She told him what she thought of that. "Lauren. Did you learn that language at my knee?"

"No, sir. I learned it when a bunch of bastards tried to tell me that as a woman, I was never going to amount to a hill of beans and that I should give up now." He grinned at her. "Tell me, Dad. How bad?"

"Shot seven times, they told us. All point blank. Twice in the chest, once in the arm, and twice in both legs. Shrapnel was taken out of your back, your chest, as well as your head. Broken leg, hand, and some damage to your lower back, but I can't get anyone to tell me what. Your mom can't get them to let her see your file either, which hasn't gone over well." Lauren nodded. She told him she'd take care of that. "I wish you would. She wants to make sure of a few things before they release you. If they release you. They're not big on giving out any kinds of timelines, are they?"

"No. Welcome to my world. And I'm assuming that they didn't tell you what happened." He said that they checked her body when they could to see the extent of her injuries or they'd not even know as much as they did. Not so much as pulling out the padding and looking, but just peaking where they could. "Where is Phillips? Has he been in to see me?"

"Yes. Mostly in the morning however. He's a very busy man, I think. He said that you're to have the best. That's what has your mom so upset. She thinks she's the best." Lauren told him she was. "She'd be happy to hear you say that. You should tell her when she comes in. It'll do her heart a world of good."

"My men." He shook his head and told her what Pete had told her about the man that she'd come in with. She knew who it had to be, and was glad to think he'd made it too. "Can you do me a favor? Can you get in touch with

Phillips? Tell him I'm up and pissy. That should bring him in."

"I'm sure."

The door opened and her mom and three armed service men came in. Lauren looked at each of them and knew that they were under orders from someone higher on the chain of command than she was. But it didn't stop her from trying.

"Soldier? Do you have any idea who the fuck I am?" All three of them nodded and stood at attention. She nearly grinned but only stared at them. "When you come into a room with a higher ranking officer, what the hell are you supposed to do?"

"We were told to keep you safe." She said nothing, and that made them both stammer out some bullshit about being under orders. "Major Burcher, we were told to keep you from talking to other civilians. And that as soon as you were...you opened your eyes, we were to stand with you until someone could come and talk to you. Sir."

"My mother and father are not civilians, soldier, and they do not understand the protocols that come with it. How would you like it if I stood near your mommy with an M-16 rifle at the ready? Not much, I'm betting. And when you address them, it's as if you're talking directly to me. Get Major General Phillips here now."

They nearly fell over each other to get out of her room. Even as the door closed behind them, Lauren knew that getting what she wanted had cost her. She slipped into the darkness even as her dad was asking her about her title.

When she woke the next time, the room was darker but not black. She saw Tony sitting in the chair using a smallish computer with earbuds in. They were alone. Instead of letting him know she was awake again, she watched him.

He'd recruited her for her first mission. He had told her that any person that was as mean as her deserved to have every shit job there was out there. And Tony had made sure she'd had some really shitty jobs too. Right up until she'd been in the right place at the wrong time.

"You going to stare at me all night, or say thank you for getting your ass out of there when I did?" Grinning, she told him to fuck off. "Such a mouth on you. Does your mom know you talk like that?"

"No. And she'd better not find out, either." He nodded but didn't move. She had expected...well, Lauren wasn't sure what she'd expected. Questions for sure. Reasons? She didn't have any of those either. Instead of asking or even telling him anything, she moved on to her parents. "My dad said you've been taking care of them very well. Thanks for that."

"They're very good people. Your father told me how he came to have you as a daughter." She didn't say anything. If her dad told him everything, she was sure that Tony would have even more questions, and she didn't want to answer them right now. "Pete is a good kid. I think he was thinking about joining up until the other morning."

"What happened?" He didn't answer her, and she looked at him. "Did you talk him out of it or did someone else? Who do I need to thank for that?"

"Your man, McCullough. He's a good man too. I'm sure you're aware of that." She was. Something flittered through her mind, but it was too painful to catch right then. "He's here too. Doing better than you, but I suspect you knew that he would be."

Tony was a cat. A tiger. She'd always thought his parents had a strange sense of humor naming him that, but who was she to argue about parents and what they did?

She'd not come from the best of them. Had only ended up with the best.

She was sure that there were people who knew what Tony was, but Lauren didn't care. Hawkins would have known. They could sort of sniff people out that were like them. But as far as she was concerned, people were people. Some were assholes, others worse, but for the most part they were just people. Lauren thought of her men, the ones that had been there with her when she'd been following orders.

"The rest? They're all gone?" He nodded. Turning away from him, she thought of the things that they'd run into the moment they'd been dropped off. "We were ambushed. But I'm sure you knew that as well. They not only knew that we were coming, but when and how many of us there was going to be. They murdered those men as surely as if the ones that gave the orders had been there with us."

"Yes, you were ambushed. And I'm trying to figure out how the hell it went down. Something wasn't right, and we both know it." He didn't elaborate and she didn't ask him how he knew. "I had to make some pretty painful calls these last few weeks. Those men didn't deserve that. Neither did you. Their parents, they have a lot of questions that I just don't have answers for."

He was keeping something from her. She knew it, and she was pretty sure that he knew she did. Tony was a straight shooter, so whatever it was, it was going to hurt her pretty badly. Not just physically but also in her head. There were too many gone for it not to be that bad.

"What do you not want to tell me, Tony?" He didn't say anything, so she turned to look at him. "Are they putting me out to pasture? Are they blaming this one on me?"

"No. They aren't blaming anyone right now. As for you being put out to pasture…do you want to be?" Lauren wasn't sure and said as much to him. "Good. Don't let it overwhelm you. But I will tell you as much as I can for now. You weren't shot—at least not only shot. We let your parents believe that because they weren't going to be happy with just telling them that you'd been hurt badly. Shrapnel hit you everywhere. The one in your chest is what we were most concerned with, but a buddy of yours came in and helped you along with that one. Victoria said you and her are now even."

Victoria was an old vampire. Someone she had befriended…well, befriended might have implied they weren't friends, but they both knew that for whatever reasons, they needed each other. Both then and off and on over the years they had come to depend on each other a great deal. Victoria would have come to her, knowing that had she been hurt, Lauren would have gone to her.

"What can you tell me? And I don't mean the bullshit stuff you're going to tell them. I want to know what happened, not the watered down version that they're going get from you." She asked him what he meant by that. "You know as well as I do that someone wanted you dead. And if I know you as well as I think I do, then you're going to keep some of the shit that went down close to your head so you can review it and work it out on your own. You no more trust them than I do at the moment. So give it to me straight."

"As soon as we landed, we knew we were in the wrong place. There was so much personnel around that it looked like a fucking convention. We had our orders, and no matter how many times I checked, no one would tell me who gave them. Not one shit hole there had any idea who had called us in, either." She thought about the building that they'd entered. "The first man through the door was Jacobs. He was ahead of me by two, maybe three steps. He just disappeared. I think he set off the chain of events unknowingly, and that's when we were hit with it. They were us, Tony. Not rebels or any other faction. They were army." Tony asked her if she knew what squad they were in. "No. I know now that we were targeted. Just not a reason for it. Do you?"

"No. All we know is that you and your men were to go in, secure the building for the next group, then stand down when they arrived. Of course when the second squad arrived, they were put in the middle of the shit storm, and six of the eleven there were killed as well." She asked him why they were there at all. "That's what we're trying to figure out. You were supposed to let them know when the building was secured. Then twenty-four hours later, they would come in. Nothing went as directed."

"And now that it went to shit, they're scrambling to figure out what to tell the public." He didn't say anything, but then he didn't have to. Lauren had been at this long enough to know a fuck job when she heard it. "How bad is it going down?"

"Your man McCullough has your back. He said that he was near you, as were the rest of the men, when the orders came in. And that they were executed with your usual flare of grace under stupidity." She could almost imagine the man saying that. He was...colorful was about the term she'd call him. "He also said that had it not been for you, things might have been worse."

"How the hell could it have gone any worse? I had nineteen men. Now I have no one." He handed her a file, and she looked at the cover. The stamp TOP SECRET was in bold red letters. "I'm not authorized to see this."

"You are now." She didn't ask, and wouldn't...not now at least. "McCullough said that you pulled them back and regrouped even when the odds were stacked poorly in your favor. You had them fire on the men there. Twenty-nine men, all from a group that isn't claiming responsibility yet. And now we both know why. They were under orders, the same as you. What do you suppose was going through their head when they realized they were firing on friendlies?"

"When we landed, our naked asses put there, I tried twice to call it in. Something was...off. I didn't like it and most of the men didn't either. Especially the ones that could smell it like yesterday's shit rags." She knew that, like other things in the army, it was a "don't tell and we won't ask" sort of mentality. So while there were shifters on her team, she doubted very much if anyone gave a shit so long as the job was done. "The orders finally came in to take the building at all costs. Secure and call. So we did."

"Do you remember who you talked to? Any name given?" She frowned. The name? Lauren laid her head back and tried to think, but it hurt. "Don't. Don't hurt yourself trying to think for now. Just tell me what you remember."

She didn't like not remembering. It was there, right on the tip of her memory. Closing her eyes, she tried to let it flow through her, and that, too, hurt. The pain washed over her, not just in her head but all over her body. Lauren could hear Tony asking her if she was all right then. Well, nothing.

~~~

Colin wasn't any happier here than he'd been back at the plant two weeks ago. But instead of hearing, "I don't know," he was hearing, "I'm not at liberty to share that information with you." Not any better at all. He looked at Hawkins when he laughed.

"You hate not being in charge and knowing it all, don't you?" Colin told him it was his job to know it all. "Yeah, well suck it up, big brother. No one is going to tell you shit. Not unless you need to know. And even then, you won't get all of it."

"I'm glad to see you having so much fun at my expense. Several days ago you were crying like a baby about how hurt you were, and now you're making fun. See if I drop everything and come here for you again." They both knew that he would. And Hawkins would do the same for him. "When do you get out of here, anyway?"

"Can't go until they release me, you know that. And I doubt it has much to do with all this shit that happened to my pretty body." No, he doubted they were holding him here just for a few broken bones that had healed the moment he woke up, and would do so faster when he was able to shift. Hawkins hadn't been able to since he woke. The first day he was awake, Colin had begged him to do so, but Phillips had told him it would not play well with the others if he was all neat and pretty. "Have you been in to see my CO yet?"

"They have a guard on the door. And every time I ask, I get the same shit. Too much pain." He'd been trying for the last few days to walk down the hall and talk to this Burcher person. Each time he'd been turned away. He wanted to thank him for getting his brother out alive, and then beat the ever loving shit out of him for letting his brother get hurt. "Do you suppose they're keeping us from him because they think he had something to do with all this?"

Hawkins just laughed, as he did every time he tried to talk to him about his commanding officer. Colin did really want to meet him. And his parents. Someone had done a bang up job on raising this man, and he wanted to tell them that. He knew for a fact that his own parents, even with what they'd had to work with, had raised them right.

When Phillips showed up ten minutes later, Colin went into the hall. He knew that he'd be asked to leave anyway, and didn't want the man to have to be polite in asking. He tried, but it was more like he was commanding him, and Colin hated that as well.

Before he was halfway down the hall, he saw a group of military men, dressed like they were going to war and armed that way as well, going toward the room he'd been told the CO was in. This was not going to be good, he knew it. Whatever was going down, blood was going to be shed.

Making his way in that direction, he paused at the nurse's station. He'd been talking to them, all the nurses and doctors, every day since he'd been there, and felt confident that they'd tell him what was going on if they knew it. Instead of finding the place a beehive of activity as it usually was, the entire area was empty. Not good, his mind told him. Not good at all.

Hawkins, something is wrong here. He asked him what was going on. *Six dressed to the teeth men are standing around the door to that CO of yours. The nurses, docs, and even the regular staff is gone. The armed guards that were out there not an hour ago are missing too. Tell that boss of yours. Shit is going down.*

The door opened behind him, and he glanced back to see Phillips coming toward him. When he stopped in front of him, he turned with his back to the men that had just moved around the corner and out of his direct line of sight. He handed him a handgun.

"You know how to use this?" His voice was low but hard. When Colin took the offered gun, he nodded. "You stay here. If they make a move, shoot for the head."

Head? He wasn't sure he could shoot someone in the head, but nodded. If this went sour—and right now, he doubted there was anywhere else for it to go—he would do what he needed. The elevator door opened to his right, and he looked at his family just as they were ready to speak.

Leave. His dad started to argue, as he always did, but Colin simply showed him the gun and he nodded. Thankfully when the door closed, Colin knew they were going to be safe. He just hoped he was as well.

"Hello, boys." None of them acknowledged Phillips as he spoke. Colin moved closer, but not close enough to actually touch them. Them not talking to Phillips...to Colin's way of thinking, that was just wrong. "You have orders to be here? If so, I'd very much like to see them."

"We don't report to you." That sounded like something someone would say to him, not to this man. But Colin stayed where he was, and so did Phillips. "If you don't want to get hurt, you should move on. We're here to work, not shoot the shit with the likes of you."

"She's armed." The first man in the group looked at Phillips when he spoke. Colin had no idea who he was talking about, but the men, all of them, looked at Phillips now. "Yeah, made sure she was as soon as she was awake. You'd not believe the red tape that was involved in getting her handgun in to her. Not to mention the seven extra clips that are within her reach. Just thought you'd like to know that in the event you're headed into that room."

"No, she isn't. We would have been told that." Phillips stepped back and waved at the door. It almost looked to Colin like he was saying, "see for yourself." "She is in no position to be armed. You're bluffing."

"Am I?" Phillips took another step back. Then in a loud voice he spoke again. "Six men, armed and covered. When they come in, fire first and we'll clean up later."

Colin started to take a step toward Phillips, sure he'd lost his mind. Then he saw the door move, swing slowly back so that it gave the appearance of welcoming them. Colin moved back, his body hard with the unknown. When the first man dropped, his head suddenly just not there, Colin stood there and watched as another man fell.

Even before the next man fell, his gun was gone. Colin looked at his brother Hawkins as he lifted the gun he'd taken from him and fired almost in the same motion. He was down then. Colin was pressed to the floor as two more were dead. The last man standing dropped to his knees just as someone came out of the room that the CO had been in. Blood spilled onto the floor in front of the last man, even as he tried to stem the flow with his hands over the hole where his knee used to be.

"Phillips?" He said he was all right to the woman standing there. Blood dripped down her arm, her head was bleeding as well, and he was sure she was only standing up because of the secure hold she had on the wall. "Mac, see to this piece of shit."

She was falling. Even before he could think that touching this woman who was armed better than his brother had been was a bad idea, he rushed forward and snatched her up in his arms. Phillips told him to get her into the room, and Colin moved there, returning her to the room that she'd just come out of.

As he laid her on the bed, all he could think about was how beat to shit she was. Blood poured from the wound on her head, there was blood on her gown, and her leg looked like she'd opened up a long gash there. He was just covering her up when she lifted her gun and put it on his forehead. This close, there was no fucking way he was going to walk away from this. But all he could think about was the look in her eye. She just simply would not care if he was dead.

He stared into the most incredible blue eyes he'd ever seen. Crystal clear with just enough blue in them to make you think of ice formations, cold winter days snuggled in bed with her, and sex. A great deal of sex. Before he could analyze what the fuck his mind was thinking, he heard that soft laughter, and then his brother's voice.

"Lauren, it's my brother." Colin watched the face of the woman when his brother spoke behind him again. "Don't shoot him. If you do, my mom is going to be really pissed, and you so don't want that coming down on your head. Lower your weapon, sir. He's a friendly."

"Hurt? You hurt?" Colin wasn't sure if she was talking to him or Hawkins, but his brother told her he was fine. "Get me something. A bullet would be fine. Hurt badly."

"Lower the gun, Lauren, and I'll call the medics in to help you. I can't until you let my brother go." She continued to stare at him, her eyes glazed with the pain she'd said she had. "Lauren, lower your weapon and I'll help you."

The gun didn't so much as lower as it dropped on her lap. She was out, her body just simply limp with unconsciousness. Colin didn't move, his hands still positioned to pull the sheet, bloodied he could see now, up and over her body. When Hawkins said his name again, he finally could pull his eyes away from her. By then, he knew what he'd been feeling.

"This is your CO?" Hawkins laughed and said it was. "Mother fuck balls. She's also my mate. Your boss is my mate. How do you fucking like that?"

Hawkins was still laughing as the nurses, now back on duty, were brought in. When Hawkins continued to laugh, not even able to talk, Colin was ready to bash his head in. Might have too, if he hadn't noticed that Hawkins was bleeding too. Hawkins was ordered to his room just as his mate was wheeled back to surgery. Colin wondered if this was just a simple nightmare. There was no way she was his mate. She was...well, more scary than his mom was.

Chapter 3

Lauren woke to find herself not only in a different room, but she was pretty sure that she was no longer in the hospital. The place looked like one of the spreads they had in girly mags at the beginning of the grocery line. Not that she'd ever read one of them or done any grocery shopping, but she'd seen them when she'd gotten herself a frozen pizza and beer, her usual dinner.

"You get hurt more than I have ever been. And you know that's a great many years." Lauren looked at Victoria. "I came when I felt your pain. I wasn't sure I was going be able to help you this time."

"I've told you before, if it's that bad, then let me go. I don't think I was ever meant to live this long anyway." Victoria only smiled and sat on the chair across from her. "You have some nice digs here. How did you manage to get them to let me go?"

"It was safer for you not to be in such a public forum. And this isn't my place. You should also know that I didn't bring you here, nor was it your pain that made me saving you so difficult. You have a mate." Lauren closed her eyes and leaned back on the most incredible pillow that she'd ever had. "Did you hear me, Lauren? You have a mate."

"Yeah, I think you've told me that cock and bull story before. How long have I been here, and when the fuck can I leave? I don't think it's any safer for me to be here than...whose house is this? Some rich fuck?" Victoria laughed as the door opened behind her.

Lauren watched the woman come in with a man whose face tugged at her memory. They were arguing, and Lauren had a sudden urge to sit up straighter and fix her hair. It wasn't the woman that had her feeling less than herself, but the man. He looked at her and her body heated.

"You're awake." Nodding at the man, she suddenly felt her temper get the better of her. It was all she could to not to snap at him for some reason. "They said you'd be out for a few more days, but then I guess you rarely do things by the book. Tony has been telling us that you're only the best at what you do because you don't follow rules. Well, I like them...rules, I mean."

"The book will get you fucking killed. And even if it doesn't, you can't always depend on a book when common sense is a better way to go. Where the hell am I?" The woman cleared her throat and Lauren, for probably the first time in her life, felt her face heat up in embarrassment. "Where the heck am I?"

"My parents' home. Mine wasn't equipped to handle the extra men that your boss insisted be with you. Hawkins is here too." Nodding, she looked at the man as he continued. "We have to talk, you and I. I think we need some ground rules before you start thinking you're in charge."

"Behave, Colin, or I'll tell your father to come up here and show her the pictures he has in his wallet. Hello dear, my name is Beatrice, but you can call me Bea. My husband is Richard, but he goes by Rich." Lauren nodded and glanced at Victoria. "Oh, I didn't see that you had company already. I'll leave you to your—"

"I must leave. I only came to tell my friend that the scales have tipped in my favor again." Victoria leaned in and kissed her on the cheek. Then she whispered in her ear. "This is your family, my friend. And that is your mate. Good luck."

Then she was gone.

Lauren looked at the woman who was staring at her and the man who was...she wasn't sure what his face looked like. Perhaps he was in pain. Or worse yet, he knew that she was his mate. Lauren shook her head as her mind started working around the implications of what she'd been told.

"Not going to happen." He nodded. "I don't think so. I have a career and a life, and you are so not fucking it up." Lauren glanced at the woman. "Can you give us a minute? I have to let this guy know that whatever crap is going on in his thick head right now is not going to happen. Not over my dead body."

"You have come pretty close to that several times now, haven't you? What the hell were you thinking, getting out of bed like you did?" She started to stand and realized that she was still armed, so she pulled out her weapon and pointed it at him. "Where the hell did you get that thing?"

"Colin, perhaps cooler heads will prevail around here." Neither of them took notice of Bea. As Colin advanced toward her, Lauren slid the bar back and ejected the round before pointing it back at him. "Colin? I think you're going about this all wrong."

"She is not going to be armed in your house. There are enough armed men running around as it is without her taking pot shots at whoever she wants." Lauren knew this was stupid on some level, but she held steady. When she stretched her neck, the pop of it was loud in the room and he stopped advancing toward her. "Put that away before I have to come over there and take it from you."

"Fuck you. You come any closer and we'll see how this ends. And as for you trying to take my gun? That's not going to happen either. You cannot outrun a bullet no matter how bossy you are to it. And I know what you think you are, and that is not on my agenda. Get out of here."

The door opened again and closed. Lauren didn't bother looking to see who had entered the play area, but held her gun steady on the man's chest. It would be a real shame to mess up this pretty room, but she would if he came any closer.

"Major Burcher, you shoot my brother and I will kill you." McCullough's voice was steady, low and full of promise. "Put the weapon down and I'll get him out of the room so that we can talk."

"I don't want to talk about this." He stepped in front of Colin and had his own weapon pointed at her. "You'll go to prison for this, Mac. You can't draw on your commanding officer. Even for what you're doing now, you will be put before a firing squad."

"You'll be dead too if you make me shoot you. I know you have a death wish, but I'd just as soon not carry it out for you. Put the weapon down and I'll get him out of here." She watched the man she'd worked with for the last sixteen years, side by side, and knew that he'd do just as he said. "You know I can do it. I've told you before what my family means to me. I *will* kill you."

She didn't move. The man behind him wanted something that Lauren didn't have to give. Not love, not romance. She didn't even own her life. The army did. Yet here she was, her weapon pointed at one of the few men that she'd ever trusted, and he was going to kill her.

"Lauren, if you don't lower your weapon, I'm gonna get killed. I'm certainly gonna get hurt, but if you hurt my family, I will die." Tearing her eyes from Colin, she asked him why. "Because if you hurt them, I'm going to attack you. And if you don't do that, the moment you lower your weapon, Colin is going to attack me for threatening you because you're his mate. Either way, I'm gonna lose some blood."

Lauren looked at Colin again. He nodded once, to no doubt confirm that what Hawkins said was true. She pointed her weapon at him then. She smiled at Colin as she spoke to Hawkins.

"All right then. I'll just shoot him and that'll solve both our problems. You'll be safe and I won't have to deal with his bullshit and aggravation." She stretched her neck, popping the tense muscles again. "I can do it, no problem."

"Don't." Colin took a step around Hawkins as he continued. "I think I might have pissed you off. I think—"

"You only *think* you pissed me off? I'm thinking, and this is only my opinion, but I'm betting pissing people off is as natural to you as it is to me." Colin told her she didn't need to be so nasty. "I give as good as I get, buster. Deal with it."

"Perhaps if we start over, with cooler heads, the guns could be put away." Bea put out her hand to Hawkins. "Hand it over, son, and I will promise Lauren will do the same."

"No, I won't. This is fucked up."

Bea turned to her with fire in her eyes. Lauren became the twelve year old again, living in the shack with her parents, and flinched back, fear making the gun in her hand tremble slightly.

"You'd rather they both die? Because as surely as we're all here, that is what will happen." She turned toward her son again. "Hawkins?"

Lauren watched Mac as he released the clip in the handle, then handed it to his mom. As he ejected the one in the chamber, never taking his eyes from her, he handed his weapon to her as well. Then Bea turned to her with her now empty hand out.

"This isn't right. I'm not one to just give up, and certainly not one to just turn over my weapon without a fight." Nothing, no acknowledgement of what they were doing to her. "He leaves. Or no deal."

"I'm not—"

"Of course. Colin, please go into the hall."

He looked murderous. Lauren wanted to stick her tongue out at him, or at the very least smirk. But she didn't think this was over, nor did she think a gun pointed at his head was gonna stop him the next time. He left, closing the door with extreme quietness.

Disarming her gun, she turned over her weapon, but kept the clip and extra casing. She looked at Bea then; her face was pained. Lauren asked her what was wrong, she'd won this round.

"I won nothing. And neither did you if you think so. You have any idea what this cost us? Me, my sons? We are not the kind of people who pull guns on each other. We are supportive, loving, and have each other's backs. And we love each other." Lauren felt the tears she'd not shed in years fill her eyes while this woman, a complete stranger, put her in her place. "What are you going to do about this, Lauren? You are the only one that can fix it."

Reaching to Victoria, she begged her to come. When she appeared in the room beside her bed, Lauren stood up. It was hard; she was still in a great deal of pain despite having the help she'd had. Nodding once to the vampire, she looked at Bea.

"Nothing. Not a damned thing. I didn't ask for this, and I have no intentions of being the mate to an arrogant ass that means less to me than I do to myself." Victoria wrapped her arms around her and Lauren continued. "You had no right to do this to me any more than he did coming in here telling me that I was stupid when I saved his fucking ass."

Bea might have spoken, but Lauren no longer cared. She wanted out, now, and when she squeezed Victoria's hand, they were no longer standing in the bedroom but in Victoria's home. The home of a very old and very wealthy vamp that was laughing at her.

"You have really fucked up this time, my friend." Lauren only sat down on the sofa that was close to her. "Yes, ma'am. Fucked up royally."

Lauren was pretty sure she was right. But for now she was safe, and so were they. Because, despite the fact that the man thought she was going to be his mate, there were people after her, and bringing the monsters to their doorstep would get them all killed.

~~~

Colin tried his best not to speak, because he knew that once he opened his mouth, he'd spew things that he could never take back. So while his mother sat on the couch and sobbed, Colin tried to think what the hell he'd done to deserve this.

"Son?" Colin looked at his dad. "You have to go and find her. The way she left, your mother is very upset and I don't care for that at all. Do you know this vampire that took her?"

"I'm sorry she upset you, Mom. I truly am." His mom looked at him and frowned. "I'll train her to not speak to you that way again. She'll apologize as well. I won't have her treating you like that."

His mom stood up and so did he. Colin towered over her, yet he felt small and helpless around her. When she slapped him, jerking his head around with a loud snapping sound, he stared at her with his mouth open as she drew back to do it again.

"You did this. You started this. She was right when she said that you had no.... What were you thinking, going in there and making a complete ass of yourself?" He started to speak but she cut him off with her hand up again. "Say one more word about training her and I will not be responsible for what I do to you. My goodness, Colin, what century do you think this is? Train her? She's not a dog or a child. We moved her here without her permission. We invaded her life. You treated her...I'm not sure what you thought you were doing, but going in there like you were some...like some...asshole, just as she called you, will not work either. Train her? Oh son, you'll be lucky if she ever comes here again."

"She was nasty to you." His mom said no more so than she'd been to her. "How do you figure that? She was all defensive as soon as we got there."

"She's military. And in the event that you missed it, she saved your life. And those of the rest of the staff in that hospital. You made it sound as if she'd been out for a Sunday stroll and spontaneously started bleeding for no other reason than to make you mad. Do you have any idea what happened to her over there? Or your brother, for that matter? Who, I might add, has said he won't return here so long as you're here. You've managed in less than ten minutes to not only alienate your mate, but your brother too." He told her no one knew what happened over there, no one would tell them anything. "I do. Most of it anyway. As does your father. What Hawkins couldn't tell us, we got when we talked to Mr. Phillips. He gave us a great deal of information too. But as I remember, you were too busy being on the phone when he was talking to us."

"I'm trying to save a business, mine and Larson's. And what did you expect me to do, simply hang up on him whenever we were not given any information that was helpful?" She only stared at him, that look in her eyes that told him he was in too deep to back out of it now. "Mom, what happened over there? Please tell me."

"We were ambushed. And I just found out why the nursing staff was gone. They were told there was an active shooter on our floor and they were escorted out. Those men had orders to kill anyone left on the floor. That would have included you, Colin." They all turned when Hawkins made his presence known. "But as for why we were there? There were nineteen of us when we went in, counting both me and Lauren. Two new blood that we picked up on the way over too. As soon as we hit the ground, we knew that we were fucked. Not only were we dropped sixteen miles from the place, but we were also dropped in the middle of a place so hostile that we were lucky to have only lost one man on the way in. And the amount of personnel...army there made us realize that we had been brought in for no reason. But as a matter of fact, we were there to be killed."

"Where?" Hawkins didn't answer him. He wasn't sure he would have except that he did finally say that it was classified. "Why were you there then? I mean, other than what you just told us?"

"A building needed to be secured for a reason I can't talk about. To be honest, I'm not sure what we were doing there. I don't want to think they brought us there to kill us, but…. We weren't normally the ones that went in to secure empty buildings, but we were told to do it, and rather than just ignoring it, we made our way to where they told us. We're the ones that go in after it's cleared to do the actual job. The army just loves to give orders that seem to make no sense. But the orders came in twenty-four hours after we were given the okay for R&R." He asked him if he was coming home on his rest and relaxation leave. "I was. All of us were. It was only going to be for ten days, but we'd been on for sixteen months. We were all looking forward to it."

"What is it you do over there, Hawkins? I'm assuming you can at least tell us that." Hawkins shook his head at his dad. "What can you tell us then, damn it?"

"We entered the building. Lauren, my commanding officer and the best in the army, said that we were to go in pairs. It was her and me together. We usually went by seniority, and I was always paired with the newer recruits. But since we, she and I, were going in first, she wanted the best with her. That was her words, not mine. As we moved through the lower part of the building, both of us knew that we weren't alone; her, by whatever ability she has that makes her scary intuitive, and me because I could smell them. Just as we were halted at the bottom of a staircase, one of our men, Jacobs, moved to go through the doorway into the next room. The blast took him out. Both Lauren and I were covered in his blood as the bomb exploded. His partner...we're not even sure what happened to him, only that we know he was killed as well." Colin sat down, his legs weak with the newfound knowledge of how dangerous his brother's job was. "Lauren and I moved as a unit, which is how we normally do things, and took out six of the men stationed all around us in seconds. It was then that we knew...that we knew who was firing on us. Two of our men were down, headshots...nothing we could do but move on. Three more were shot just as we took out four more of their guys. We were surrounded. And we knew in that moment that we were set up, and that we more than likely weren't going to make it out alive."

Colin watched Hawkins as he relived what had gone down. His mom held onto their dad, and even he looked a little frightened at what they were hearing for the first time. At least Colin was.

"I was shot in the arm, Lauren twice in her leg, but that was not the extent of our injuries. We'd both been hit by bombs going off. Some shrapnel hit both of us badly. She didn't stop, didn't even pause as we moved on, and blood stained the floors as we took out two more together. Grenades were thrown at us, taking out four more of our team. Three of them were shifters and didn't stand a chance with the carnage that happened to them. Lauren moved on, took out three more as she ordered me to stay back, take care of the wounded, and undress the dead." Colin asked him what that meant. "Dog tags. We took one set and left the other with the bodies. Fat fucking lot of good it did us to leave the bodies behind. When they blew the building, there was nothing left for us to send home."

Colin had heard that. That most of the dead they had been unable to retrieve. He'd not thought of what that had meant until now. Nor how lucky they all were that Hawkins and Lauren were even here.

"By the time I caught up with Lauren, I'd been shot twice more. Nothing serious this time thanks to being a cat, but she'd been hurt too. In the chest. And six more of our men were gone. We were down to seven then. Two of them were wounded more than we were and weren't going to make it out. Dragging them to the doorway to get them out of the building and hopefully to safer grounds, we heard the jets coming in." Hawkins said nothing as he sat there, his face washed with pain. Not just of his body, which had pretty much healed when he'd been able to shift, but at the loss of his friends and comrades as well. "Three seconds, no more after we heard them, she ordered me out. I tried to argue with her that it was unsafe for her to remain, but she said that I had to pull the others, even if it was only their bodies, out. She even said that if I got hurt...she said if I got hurt...."

He broke down then, sobbing hard, and Colin got up to hug him. As the rest of his story poured out, Colin knew that he had to find Lauren, if for no other reason than to thank her for what she'd done for them.

"She told me if I got hurt or killed, she'd have to tell my family. The family that she'd heard so much about over the years that she felt like she knew them as well as I did. And telling them...having to tell them that I was killed in the line of duty would be harder for her than anything she'd ever have to do again." Colin held him tighter after that. But Hawkins pulled away and looked at him. "I was standing there, debating whether or not to leave her, when the bomb exploded beside her. She was flying through the air, her body bloodied and broken, when I felt the shrapnel hit me everywhere. I had been standing there, right next to her, not seconds before. Had she not sent me away, ordered me to do as she fucking said, I'd be dead. Right now, I'd not even be enough to bury, and she saved me. And you made me pull my weapon on her because you're an ass."

Hawkins left them then. Just, without another word, moved out of the room and then out of the house. Colin heard the car start—the one of Larson's that Hawkins had been using since he'd been able to drive again—and the muffler was loud. As the gravel sprayed against the house Colin sat down, realizing that he had really fucked up this time.

"You know this vampire?" Colin told his dad that he didn't. "Then I would suggest you find out what you can. Because whether or not you care about what you did to her, your brother won't forgive easily for what you made him do today."

"I don't forgive me well either, Dad." He looked at his father then, tears staining his face. "I'm a monster. I have always been one."

"Not a monster, no. But the oldest, and for some reason you've had it in your head that it's your way or the wrong way. I tried my best to temper that with humor, but it never stuck." Colin said nothing, thinking of all the times when his dad had joked about a simple mistake he'd made, and Colin only being pissed at how stupid he thought his father was. All along, his dad had been brilliant and tried to teach him the same things.

"Do you know how to get in touch with Phillips? Maybe he can help me." His dad only shook his head. "Then who do I have to beg to make this right?"

"Make it right for who?" He asked his mom what she meant. "You're willing to fix this, and I'm glad, but who are you working to fix this for? You have a mate that would just as soon shoot you as to look at you, a brother that can't stand to be in the same room with you, and your parents that feel like failures for the way you've treated them both. Or for you, Colin, because you don't like being in the wrong?"

"For all of us. I was wrong. And I'm going to...I don't know what I'm going to do to make it up to the people that I love, but I feel that I have to start with Lauren. She's going to...I failed her far worse than you think you did me. Which, you didn't. You tried, but I was too pig headed to see it until now." His mom said he'd get no arguments from her. "I'm sorry. I promise you, I'll take care of this, all of it."

"You'd better, son. You won't get another chance at this. Not just with your brother, but your mate as well." He nodded at his dad as he stood up. "Lauren's parents live around here somewhere. Don't know them, but then we don't really socialize that much anymore. Burcher. I think they have a farm not far from Parker."

Colin decided to start there. Perhaps they'd know where Victoria took Lauren. He wondered, too, about Lauren's parents. He hoped that they'd give him a chance if Lauren had spoken to them since he'd made a total ass of himself.

Chapter 4

Lauren was walking—working up to running as gently as she could without hurting more—around the open field when she saw the big cat standing in the way. It had been a long time since she'd seen either of her parents as a cat, or Pete for that matter, but they sure were bigger than she remembered. This male was more than likely Pete, as he was bigger than their dad. She wondered fleetingly if she should have been afraid, but only smiled at the silly thought.

"You scared me." He stood there and she started to walk again. "Just so you know, I've got men on the property today fixing the last of the flooring in the house. So if you see them, don't scare them off. It was hard enough getting them to come out here on such short notice."

Pete loped alongside her as she tried to walk a little faster. It was hard at first, getting her body to move again, but once she was going the stiffness would usually work its way out. She told him this as they moved down the path that she'd been working on.

"I have the house nearly finished. Thanks so much for looking in on it while I was gone. The furniture in the bedrooms looks good." She walked a little more, then stopped. Lauren knew she was pushing herself, but she needed to get back to her job. Someplace other than here. As she sat down on the log next to her, Pete came to lay at her feet. "What's up, big guy? Dad pissy with you again? I told you to back off with the smart mouth shit. He's not gonna take it like he does with me."

Running her hand over his head, she felt him purr. His body leaned heavily into hers, and she had to push him back or be knocked off the log. Before she could tell him to settle down, she was on her back and he was over her. Only it wasn't Pete, but Colin. The change to human startled a scream from her.

"I won't hurt you." She told him to get off her. "No. I don't think so. You see, if I get up, I'm going to be exposed to you. Like I'm naked exposed."

Her body chilled, then warmed. As he moved, his hardness adjusting to fit over hers better, she felt his cock as it touched the top of her naked thigh. Her shorts, not at all modest anyway, were riding up as he moved again.

"Stop moving, damn it." He chuckled at her as he leaned into her throat. Jerking his head up off her, she lifted her head to butt him with it when he moved back, bringing his groin deeper into her pussy. "Let me up, at least, while you find your clothing and get dressed."

"I need to talk to you." She struggled to get out from under him when he stilled her with his hand to her hip. "You keep moving like that and I'm going to come all over you. And that would be such a shame, since I'd like nothing more than to be buried deep inside of you right now."

"We're not having sex." Her body screamed at her that she was so fucking wrong. He must have thought so too, because he rocked into her again. "Don't do that, Colin. I don't even like you."

"I know, and that's my fault too." He just lay there, his body pinning hers down to the ground, while he looked at her. "I want to talk to you anyway. If I shift and go meet you at your home, will you allow me to talk to you?"

"I don't have anything to say to you." He didn't move. "Why do you even care? It's not like we have mated or anything. Your kind can go for years knowing their mate and not going insane when you can't have her. Not like wolves."

"You know a great deal about us. I'm assuming that's because of who your stepparents are." She told him they were her parents. "I talked to Peter and Mary this morning. They told me who you were. And why you're human. I was surprised about that. I just assumed they were humans too. I'm glad that they took you in."

Lauren told him to get off her. He moved then, his back to her, while she tried to regain control of her emotions. They'd been a little haywire lately, and she thought it was all because of this man.

"You had no right to go to them demanding answers." He told her that he'd not demanded anything. But that he'd been polite. "You don't know how to be polite. You order people around to your way of thinking, and damn them if they don't do as the high and mighty McCullough says. What are you doing here anyway?"

"I came to talk to you. Mostly to beg you to forgive me." She didn't say anything. There was nothing to forgive, really. "I'm going to shift and go to get dressed. Can I go to your house?"

"I have to finish this walk." He said he'd walk with her. "No. You won't. I want you to leave me alone. I have to get my body back in shape before they'll let me rejoin the service. I have nothing here to hold me, and I'm going back."

Colin turned and looked at her, then let his cat take him. She sat there for several minutes longer thinking about what the doctor had really told her yesterday, and not what she'd told her parents. She didn't want to think about what had been done to her, nor what was still happening to her poor beaten body.

"You won't be able to go back on active duty, at least not what you've been doing up until this happened, Lauren. You have three pieces of metal in you that could move and kill you at any moment. Recruiting will be better suited to you now if you want to stay in for your retirement, but knowing how badly you were hurt and what you did, I'm sure there can be special jobs someone like you can do now." She asked him what kind of special job he was talking about. "No more people firing at you. One where you don't have to wear a great deal of weight to move around. Your vision is off too. You won't be as expert at firing a weapon as you had been. And then there is the metal I was talking about. The one in your back is close to your spine. A wrong move and you'll be in a wheel chair with someone cleaning your feeding tube for the rest of your life. And the one in your leg could shift as well and you'd lose your leg. I'm not sure why the doctors didn't take it out in the first place, but I intend to find out."

Lauren had a feeling that whatever the reason had been for it, it wasn't really going to help her all that much. She was grounded. And she was pretty sure that she wasn't going to last long in the civilian world. Getting up, she started out on her walk again, trying not to think about how much pain she was in.

Her legs had cramped up again, so she had to limp for a while before she could get moving. Her left leg was stiff most of the time, and failed to do what she wanted it to do most of the other times. Her fingers were too sore some mornings to even zip up her pants, and tying her boots was too much effort as well.

By the time she got back to her house, not only was Colin there and dressed, but two of the men she had walking the perimeter for her were on the porch talking to him.

"Major." Nodding at the man to her right, she stared at Colin while he explained what they'd found. "The northern part of the property had a break in the fence. We're seeing to that now. And those people you had us looking into, they're still where you said they'd be. Not much of a mover, are they?"

"No. So long as they can order what they want, they won't do anything else. They have two days left to get out. If they're there after that, I want you to get them out any way you see fit." The second man laughed a little and she turned to him. "You think something is funny?"

"No ma'am. Yes ma'am. What I mean is, those people, I was thinking that they're the most complaining people I ever saw. Even when they got it in the lap of luxury, like my grand mammie used to say, they still find fault with their arrangements." She told them again what she wanted, then looked back at Colin, asking why he was allowed to be there. "He told us he was your mate."

The couple that were staying at the other end of her property needed to be moved soon. She'd found them there almost as soon as she'd gotten back to this house. And twice now she'd talked to them, and both times they'd had some reason why they weren't able to move on. Squatters were hard to evict once they set up a base point. And from what she could tell, they'd been there for some time.

"He thinks he is, but I'm not mate to anyone."

Neither man said anything as she told them she had it now. Moving by the three of them, she entered her home just as one of the workers came out of the dining room. He looked...well, guilty came to mind. Before she could find out what he'd been up to, Colin came in the house behind her and wrapped his arms around her waist.

Heat didn't just touch her but seemed to consume her. The man, the worker, stared at her and Colin like he was going to have a quiz later and they were his cheat sheets. As Colin's hand moved up her waist to just under her breast, Lauren felt her heart rate triple. The moan that escaped her lips hummed out what she was feeling. Then the man in front of her laughed.

"Pretty good setup you got here, Lauren." Her body went from heated too cold in just that second. Grabbing Colin's hand, she shoved him back and to the floor even as the man reached into his jacket. Her own gun was out and at his head before he cleared whatever he'd been reaching for. "I wasn't gonna hurt you. I was sent here by Phillips. I was giving you my orders, ma'am."

She reached into his pocket where his hand was still resting and felt the gun even before he moved. He jerked his weapon out and was pointing it at her even as she kicked out. Pulling the trigger on her own weapon as they both moved only resulted in her wall being shot to fuck and the guy falling backward from the impact of her kick. His weapon went flying across the room just out of his reach as she tried to move without screaming in pain. Just as she was ready to fire again, Colin, as the big cat, was on the intruder's chest with his mouth over his throat. Lauren slid to the floor, her knees suddenly too weak to hold her up.

"Ma'am?" The voice behind her had her turning and firing again. The curse words that came from the other room might have been funny had she not still been running on pure terror and pain. The man had been there to kill her was all her mind could focus on, beyond how badly she was hurt again. "It's Roger, ma'am. The man who you just saw on the porch. I'm a friend of Colin's. A cat too."

"What the fuck do you want? Christ. Do you want to borrow a cup of sugar or some shit? Just so you know, I'm in no mood to be social." She thought she heard him say no shit, but he spoke again before she could ask him.

"Colin wants me to tell you what he's saying so you can tell the fool under him. Not his words, mind you, but I can't...you're a ma'am even if you scare the crap nuggets out of me." She looked back at Colin, who was still holding down the piece of shit who'd started this all. "I'm gonna come on in there. For the love of James and Sandra, please don't be shooting me dead."

The younger of the two men came into the room with his hands way up over his head. Putting her gun in her lap but not letting it go just yet, she asked him who James and Sandra were.

"My son and daughter. I just don't want to leave them without a daddy too." He moved completely into the room then, and she could see that the man was really afraid. Not that she blamed him. It had been pretty intense for those few seconds. "You gonna shoot me?"

"Not if you don't make me." She nodded for him to put his hands down. "Tell me what he's saying and we'll go from there. Just don't...please don't make any kind of sudden moves. I'm running on low fuel for stupidity right now."

"Colin said thanks first of all. For not killing me when you had the chance. I'm real grateful for you not killing me too. Like I said, I got me a couple of kids at home, and they already lost their momma." Lauren smiled but said nothing. "This man...Colin wants to know if he needs to have his throat ripped out. Colin said to tell you he'd do it, no problem. I'm pretty sure he'd do it too. Never seen him so pissed before."

The low growl from Colin had her looking at him again. Roger told her that he didn't want him to elaborate, just tell her what he said. Again, she had the urge to laugh but only nodded.

"His brothers are on their way. He said to tell you not to kill any of them either. His mom and dad are coming in the car, but they'll be people, human looking I guess. They were headed out anyway and are on their way here to have a look around." She asked him what they were looking for. "He wants to make sure there ain't no more idiots around."

She took her cell phone out of her pocket and called Phillips. He answered the phone laughing, and she cut him off. "There is a man in my dining room with Colin at his throat that claimed that you sent him."

"I'm assuming that you don't believe him. And by at his throat, I can also surmise that Colin isn't giving him a hug." She told him he was right on both accounts. "Tell me what he looks like. And no, I didn't send anyone to you. When I get there, and I'm on my way, we'll work out a system that you won't have to guess the next time."

"Big, stupid looking brut. Not very quick on his feet by the way, and he knew my name." Roger spoke then. "And apparently he's a bear shifter. Colin can...I guess taste him."

"Christ. Colin will be able to tell if he's lying then. Ask him if his name is Penick. Then check him for a tat on his upper arm. It says mother, but spelled with an *a* instead of an *o*."

She moved, her body hurting more from the two falls she'd had today than anything she'd felt in a few days. Groaning as she reached for the knife in her shoe, she cut away the sleeve of Penick's shirt and sat back down. The pain wasn't just hurting her now, but she was afraid she was going to be sick with it. She asked the man if his name was Penick and Roger confirmed it.

"The tat is there. Who the hell...? Never mind. Colin said that he's him too, that he's not lying to me." Leaning against the wall behind her, she nearly closed her eyes when Philips started cursing. She smiled again...twice in one day she'd made a man curse like she did. "Tony, I'm fading fast here. It's been a very long morning and I'm hurting like a motherfucker. Who is he, and should I just let Colin kill him? It would make me feel better if I could and put his head on a pike out front for other would be assassins to see when they think about coming here."

"I have a transport four minutes out. If you have to kill him then so be it, but I'd prefer that you waited." Lauren told Colin and Roger laughed.

"He said to tell you that he's getting a cramp in his mouth, so if the man dies because of a muscle spasm, it's good to know he's not going to go to prison for it." Lauren nodded, too sick now with whatever was going on in her body to care at the moment. "Ma'am, Colin wants to know if you're going to be all right."

"No. I'm sick." She leaned over then, her belly finally catching up to whatever was wrong. And as she started to throw up again, she heard doors opening and closing and almost hoped they were there to kill her. When she was lifted up, Lauren looked into the face of Colin and wondered briefly where Penick was.

"Hawkins has him. Let it go, Lauren. Just let the pain take you away." Sounded like a good idea, and she let it swallow her up.

~~~

Tony watched the team as they cleaned up the mess. One of them was bagging up her vomit, and another one was watching the entire procedure with his gun pointed at the man. It was tense there for a little while. Colin's family had gathered their wagons around Lauren, and it had taken him showing up before anyone could get into the house without bloodshed. Tony was kind of glad for it really. If anyone needed watching over it would be Lauren.

Colin came into the room with ill-fitting clothing on and asked to speak to him. Right now it was the last thing he wanted to do, explain to this man what he thought, but he nodded and followed him to the study that was still under construction.

"She's resting now. I gave all the meds I could find in her bathroom to that guy. Was it necessary to have someone with him with a firearm?" Tony told him it was for now. "Why? What do you think is going on?"

"She told me yesterday morning that she was getting sicker. Lauren never complains. I mean, even with a knife wound in her side, she only said that it pulled...never mind. She never complains. So when she told me that she was sick, I set her up an appointment with the company docs. She was to see them again tomorrow." Colin asked him if he thought she was being poisoned. "Yes. I do. I don't know why, but yes. Whoever this is, they're working hard to have her dead. I'm going to put your brother in protective custody too, as a matter of fact."

"I'm going where she is." Tony started to tell him that was a bad idea. "You either make this work for me or I'll hurt you. I've just had to pin a man to the floor and wait for you to come and get him rather than just kill him and bury him in the back yard for no one to find. Either make it so I can be with her, or you'll be the first one I bury on this property."

It wasn't a threat—though it was a good one—but a full out promise. And he had a feeling that the man would do it too. Just as he was ready to call his bluff, even if he thought he could, the door behind him opened and there stood Peter Burcher with his son.

"Where is she?" Colin told him she was upstairs in bed and his mom was with her. Peter looked at Colin. "You did this? You hurt her?"

"No, sir. Not this time. I promise you." Peter watched him for several seconds, but then looked at Tony again. "He didn't hurt her either. There are some pretty shitty men after her. He's been taken in and we're doing all we can to make sure that she's not in this situation again. I assure you."

"What are you going to do to protect her?" Tony started to answer the big man, but before he could form a thought, Colin spoke.

"Everything within my power. My family will as well. If you could lend a hand, I'd really appreciate that too."

Peter seemed to calm a little. Tony wondered if either of them thought that Lauren could easily protect them when she was healthy. But right now, she did need the help. And he was going to give it all to her.

When his cell phone rang, he felt a shiver of apprehension run up his spine. He knew that ring tone over even his own children's. Walking out of the room and onto the deck behind the house, he answered the president's call.

An hour later, feeling like he'd been run through a ringer, he sat down on the large wheel that held wiring at one point. He knew that Lauren had been having work done on this place, but he'd not had any idea how extensive it was. Looking up when the door opened behind him, he looked at Colin and figured now was as good a time as any to tell him what he'd been told.

"A group has claimed responsibility for killing Lauren's men. They're a militant group that says that no woman should be allowed to be in the armed forces, and they certainly shouldn't be in charge of a group of men. This particular group of ass wipes have just made it perfectly clear that they're not going to stop until every woman in the service of their country is dead." Tony looked at Colin. "They killed two women this morning by bombing the recruiting office that they were working in. Two more were killed yesterday when the bar they were in, having drinks after a long week, was also bombed."

"She's not going to be happy about any of this." Tony thought that was a gross understatement. "What do we do now? Lauren doesn't strike me as one to let others keep her safe. And I don't think I can do this on my own. My brother told me some of what happened to them."

"Lauren doesn't follow orders. Not usually when she thinks she's right. And so you know, most of the time she is. But when she was sent there, I knew something was off and had been working on seeing who had put the order in for her and her men to be there. I'm still looking, and now…well, now I have answers I think no one is going to like." Colin asked it if was true that Lauren and the president were friends. "Yes. It's true. And the reason is classified, but I've been given permission to let you know why and anything else you want to know too. She saved his life. Not just his, but his son's and wife's as well. A formal reception, in Lauren's honor, was to take place the next night. Lauren had been invited to have dinner with the family before it started, for them to get comfortable with each other. But she showed up twenty minutes early with your brother. While there, she made her way to the kitchen to see if her old friend was still working there. She walked in on a shit storm and killed nine people before they made their way to the president's suite. Where we all assumed these men planned to kill the president."

"When?" Tony told him. "I don't remember seeing anything about that. I mean, that's about the time that Hawkins started disappearing for longer and longer periods of time."

"You wouldn't have either. And yes, Hawkins had only been in the service with Lauren for three weeks; he was there with her as her escort when things went to shit. They were friends, meeting up when he came to the recruitment meetings before he got out of high school." Tony watched the man's face. If he was pissed about his brother seeing Lauren, he didn't show it. "They were friends and nothing more. But when she could, she recruited him to her team. He's been there since. A valued member, I might add too."

"I know that they're friends. I've seen how close it is too. And even if they were more, I'd know that too." He supposed he would. From all accounts, Colin was a man who got answers. "What else do I need to know?"

"I'm to stop at nothing to keep Lauren and your family safe."

Tony nodded and waited for the questions he was sure were going on in Colin's head. Instead, Colin surprised him again by only looking out over the field and not saying anything for several moments.

"Her parents, her biological parents, what do you know about them?" He told him they were dead. "Did she do it? Peter thinks she might have."

"No. She didn't have anything to do with their deaths." Tony waited for the next question and when it came, he was ready. "Victoria killed them both. Not long after Lauren ended up at the Burcher home and became a part of their family, Victoria had a run in with the Richards, Lauren's parents. Victoria didn't know who they were, but they had...hurt her, then tied her to a wall to let her die after taking all the money and other valuables from her. The sun had already started to do its business on her when Lauren found her. All Lauren did was cut Victoria free of the stakes that held her. Two days later, the Richards were found...I think the word destroyed would best describe what had happened to them."

"Do I want to know what was done to them?" Tony assured him that he did not. "Peter told me how he found her. That the place she was living in wasn't fit for an animal, much less a child. He said that they adopted her and changed her name. There's more to that story too, isn't there?"

"Yes. But it's not my story to tell you. I'm sorry." Colin nodded. "You're here because you're her mate, right? I've heard a little about you and your family from Hawkins. He talked about you guys all the time."

"Yes, I'm her mate, but I was…I'm an ass, and I said some things to hurt her and my family. I'm here to see if she'll forgive me." Tony started to tell him good luck with that when Colin continued. "I doubt very much she will. I wouldn't if I was her. But I'm going to try. Today, when I saw her, all I could think about was how I was going to save her from herself. Now I'm thinking she can save me if someone else comes here. She's not what I thought of when I thought about a mate. I'm trying to change my ways of doing things before she murders me."

Tony thought the boy was on the right path. "You'll do good to tell her that. Just like you said to me. Lauren does not suffer fools well and she hates a liar. She has this uncanny ability to know when you are lying too." He looked out over the same field. "She found out yesterday that she and the service must part ways. The president just told me she's a lifer no matter what. You should think of that when you talk to her. Lauren and the army are one. And very little will come between her and that." He looked back at Colin before continuing. "Something is off, Colin. She's been sick, and in a great deal of pain. More than I think she should be for having a vamp save her ass. But…I'm having some tests done on her vomit. When I get them, I'll let you both know."

"I'd appreciate that. I'll have my brother Boyd look into a few things too. Him I trust." So did Tony, but he didn't say anything. "You need me, I'll be here with her. For as long as she'll let me."

Tony didn't think that would be long, but he liked the man and hoped they could work it out. At least long enough for him to figure out what the fuck was going on anyway.

Chapter 5

Lauren looked at the list of drugs that had been in her system and the things they could do to her. Nineteen drugs in the three pills she was supposed to take, none of them what they were supposed to be prescribed for, had been poisoning her for several days. The doc—not a company doctor this time—told her that the only reason they hadn't killed her was because she'd been given something to counteract it in a way. Vampire blood had saved her.

Colin was sitting in the chair closest to the window, and Tony was standing by the fireplace. The room, for all intents and purposes, had been planned to be her office. Now, she thought, it would make a good dining room. She had no idea why that thought popped into her head. She supposed it had to do with the amount of stress she was dealing with.

"Do you know who did it?" Tony told her that the prints on the bottle beside hers were Penick's. "So he'd been in this house before yesterday."

Not a question, but Tony said he had been. "More than once, from the looks of things. The men I had come in, while you had your beauty sleep, scanned each room and found over three dozen cameras, and a dozen more on the outside. We think that when you came in that day, he'd been doing some adjustments. You and Colin caught him off guard."

Lauren glanced at Colin and then looked at Tony again. He was making her nervous the way he just kept watching her. As if he was ready for her to fall apart or pull a gun on him again. Her weapons were all over the house now, having been placed by Hawkins when he'd brought her a few extra clips.

She was still thinking about Colin when she heard him laugh. How she knew it was him and not Tony was beyond her, but when she looked at him again, she realized that Tony had left and Colin was sitting in the chair he'd been in.

"What's so funny? And don't get too comfortable here. I don't want you around." He only leaned back in the chair and said nothing. She could do that too, go for hours without speaking, but for some reason he made her squirm. And Lauren didn't care for the feeling. Then he started talking to her. Not at her as he'd been doing before today, but to her.

"When I found out that you'd been poisoned, I wanted to go and find this Penick person and kill him. But Tony assured me that he'd be more useful alive than dead. But that didn't lessen the fact that I still want to kill him." She asked him why he'd even care. "I'll get to that. My mother slapped me, did you know that?"

"I didn't have anything to do with that. Besides, I'm pretty sure she wants to knock me around a little too. For a mom, she's pretty mean." He just grinned at her. "Why did she finally get around to slapping you?"

"Yeah, I wondered that too when I got over being pissed about it. Not why she hit me — she told me that — but why it had taken her so long to get around to doing it. Do you want to know what I came up with?" She told him she had an idea that his mother loved him. "She does. And that is why she hit me. I think I drove her to it."

"You normally this quick on your feet for getting things in that thick head of yours?" He didn't answer her. "I don't want you here. Someone is trying to kill me, and it would be better if you were not here."

"I'm not going anywhere. That is if you'll let me stay." She started to tell him she could take care of herself better without him there, but he started talking again. "A few days ago I would have told you that I was staying here to keep you out of harm's way. But I've come to realize that you're much more capable of keeping yourself safe, and me too, than I'd ever be. Even as beat to shit as you are and taking all kinds of meds that should have killed you, you managed to not just save your own ass but mine too."

"What's happened to you? I mean, are you some pod person? Or are you trying to fuck with my head and convince me that I'm off my noodle and need you here?" He told her that he was just him with a better outlook on things. "Yeah, well, people don't change like this overnight. I'm sure that in a few hours you'll see that you're being weird and start giving me orders again. I don't take orders well."

"So I heard." She felt her face heat up when she thought of all the times she'd told Tony to fuck off over the last few hours. "That man, the one that was here today, he said he'd been sent by Phillips. Why would he say that when it would be easy for you to check out?"

"We would have been dead before I could find out. And he would have killed us both, just so you know. No witnesses is better than taking a chance that someone can identify you later." She thought of something then. "You said he was a bear. He could have told someone else that you were here and that we're onto them. You might be in danger even now. It might be too late for you to run."

"Good point. He might have told whoever sent him that I was here. And that you're involved with me." Lauren told him she wasn't involved with him. "We could be. But I'm not going to rush you. I don't want you to draw a gun on me again. Twice is more than enough for me to get that you can and will kill me."

"I'm not...you said you talked to my parents. You have to know what kind of childhood I had." He said that he did. "And you should also know that the apple doesn't fall far from the tree. I'm like them in so many ways."

"Peter and Mary are good people. You'd be lucky to be just like them." She told him that wasn't who she was talking about. "The people who brought you into this world have nothing to do with the person you've become. You did that all on your own. You're smart, well respected, and work hard. Those are not qualities that those other people gave you."

"You're missing the point here." He told her he didn't think so. "Are you always this stubborn? I thought you were turning over a new leaf or some other bullshit."

"I have. Because right now, every part of my being wants to get up, strip you down to your bare skin, and taste every inch of you before I lay you back over that bed in the other room and plow you hard enough to make you come a dozen or so times before I release inside of you. Then when you're lying there, hopefully sated, I can roll you to your back again and eat your pussy until you're ready for me again." He leaned back further in the chair and stroked his cock, which was straining at the zipper. "I'm hard, needy, and want to taste you so badly that my mouth is watering for it. And now I can smell you. You're wet, aren't you?"

"Don't do this." She watched him as he unbuckled his belt and then his pants button. As he lowered the zipper slowly, she licked her lips. He was making her crazy, and she was pretty sure he knew it. When he was free, his cock thick and straining from his groin, he fisted himself as he watched her.

"Come here. Take me in your mouth, Lauren." She shook her head, and he cupped his balls through his pants. "Please? I want to feel your pretty mouth on me. Feel you slide me down the back of your throat while I come."

She was moving before she could tell him no again. As she knelt in front of him, taking his cock in her own hands, he lifted his hips up and pulled his pants down to his thighs. She pulled them the rest of the way off him and tossed them behind her.

Her fingers didn't fit around him, he was so thick. His slick precum was making her mouth water more as she moved her hand up and down him. Watching him, she stuck out her tongue and licked his crown. He growled low when she lifted her head from him.

"Suck me, Lauren. Christ, take me please." She moved her mouth over him, and he lifted his hips up and filled her throat. Swallowing past the gag response, she cupped his heavy balls in her hand while he fucked her mouth. "Christ, yes. I'm so close, baby. Stop now or I'm going to come in your mouth."

Her head was suddenly jerked off him and she reached for him again, but he pulled her up, standing her in front of him as he tore her clothing from her. He'd never moved off the chair, and his cock hung heavily between his thighs as the tearing sound made her body overheat and needier than she'd ever been. When she was naked, he pulled her body to his mouth, sucked her clit into his mouth, and bit down.

She screamed out her release. Lauren could not have stopped it, even on threat of death. When he stood up, pulling her along behind him, all she could think about was his cock and that he was going to fuck her soon. As they entered her bedroom, he turned them as soon as the door was closed and lifted her by her ass until she was at eye level with him, his cock at her entrance.

"Say it." She shook her head. "Tell me that you belong to me and no other. Tell me, Lauren, so that I can take you. Fill you."

"I belong to no one." She moved her hips then, taking his cock into her enough that she came again. "Fuck me, Colin. Fuck me now."

He slammed forward, taking her breath away in the process. As soon as he pulled free of her and turned them, she was sobbing for him to give her his cock again. Instead, he dropped her on the bed and pulled his shirt off, but didn't touch her.

"I'm going to come. Right now, I'm going to jerk off while you lay there." She started to reach for him when he told her to stop. "If I come on you or in you, you're mine whether you say it or not."

His hand moved up and down his shaft. Precum didn't just spill from his tip but was a steady stream now. She started to beg him to take her, tell him whatever he wanted to hear just so she could feel him inside of her when he came.

Streams of his come touched her face. Her breast burned with it. As he continued to come, spraying her body and face with his cum, she rubbed it over her, loving the feeling that she got when it warmed her skin. Then she was on her back, his cock hard as before as he moved over her.

"I can't wait." Nodding, she spread her legs for him. His cock burned at her pussy. "Christ, I need you."

He fucked her slowly, his body moving over hers as his hands seemed to be everywhere. His mouth followed the path of his fingers as he pulled at her nipples, suckled at her navel, and even bit down on her hips. He sucked at her breasts over and over, pulled them until she nearly screamed at him to finish her. Her breasts were on fire for him. No matter what he did, it wasn't enough.

Every time she was close to coming again, he'd move, pause, or nip her in a way that had her body humming but not coming. When he buried his mouth over her throat, sucking hard on her pulse there, she curled her fingers into his hair and held him, needing him to bite her now more than she needed her next breath.

"Say it now." She wanted to tell him no, that she'd never say it, but he licked her there, heating her flesh like he'd set fire to her. "Say it and I'll give it all to you."

She wanted to deny him. Tell him to fuck off. But he moved his hips and lifted her leg so that it wrapped around him. When her other leg seemed to have a mind of its own and did the same, she rolled her hips up to meet every one of his downward thrusts until he stopped. He watched her face as he begged her again to say it.

"I fucking hate you right now." He grinned. "I belong to you. I don't like you, but I belong to no other."

He bit her then, sank his teeth so deeply into her throat that she saw stars, sure that he'd torn her throat out as his cock moved inside of her faster and faster. But instead of being painful as she'd thought it would be, it brought her, three times as a matter of fact, each climax building on top of the one before. Then when he drew her blood, sucked on the wound he'd made, Lauren came so hard that stars danced behind her eyelids, and then...nothing.

~~~

Colin wasn't sure what to do with himself. He had just checked on Lauren again, and she was still sleeping soundly. He wanted to join her, but was afraid that she'd kill him in his sleep. He'd just made her his mate, and he was pretty sure that she'd only let him because he'd made her need him. Smiling, he thought of how needy he'd been too.

Going into the well-stocked kitchen, he started pulling out the ingredients to cook. He wasn't sure what he wanted to cook, but the thought of his mom's cookies with chocolate chips, the only thing in the world she could make, seemed to leap out to him when he thought of something comforting for Lauren. He also found a well-stocked freezer and pulled out two thick steaks. He was putting in some potatoes to bake when Boyd contacted him.

I have the results of the meds that were in her system if you want them. I know the other guy did their tests, but you asked me to look too. He told him he did. *You're not going to believe what I found. I mean, the tests are pretty close, but it's the amounts of each one that has me scared shitless for you and her. Did they mention something called pentobarbital or pentobarbitone?* Colin said that he didn't think so, but he might have missed it. *How about something called Nembutal?*

No, nothing like that. What does it do to her? I'm assuming that it's not a drug you can find out on the shelves of the local drug store. Boyd laughed and said no. *What could it have done to her then?*

In higher doses it causes death by respiratory arrest. They use it in some prisons that perform executions. Unless you're looking for it when death occurs, it's not going to show up. Colin paused in putting cream in the batter for the cookies as Boyd continued. *There were high doses of it in those drugs she was taking. Whoever made the cocktail for her, they knew what they were doing. And I don't mean your normal run of the mill doctor either. This person had knowledge.*

Turning when he heard Lauren come in the room, he reached out and pulled her body to his. He'd come close to losing her even before he'd had her. Holding her, he told his brother that he'd get back to him and told Lauren what he'd found.

"So they want me dead, but not make a big deal out of it. I don't understand that thinking. Why take out my entire team like that, then go in the back door to kill me off here? And what sort of claim could they make unless someone knew to look for the poison?" He loved the way her mind worked, and he told her that. "Thanks, but you should know that this is not going to get you out of the shit storm you caused by getting naked with me."

"You're very beautiful naked, I'd like to say." She told him to fuck off, something that she said quite often. He changed the subject as he finished the cookie batter. "I love this house. And this kitchen. I have a place of my own—well, we do now—that has a nice place to cook in, but not like this. Do you cook at all?"

"No. I hate it. I guess it stems from getting my food from a package for most of my life. And if you tell me you cook, I might be willing to let you live here. At least for the next few days." She paced the kitchen, and he tried his best to stay out of her way. "Back to this report. Does anyone besides the two of us know that your brother did this? I mean, it could end badly for him if word got out."

"No. I asked him to have a look at the stuff I was able to gather up before anyone came here. He did it at his lab in his offices." He wondered aloud if he should put someone on his brother to watch over him.

"Already done. And only people I can trust too. You should also know that these drugs, they won't show up on any report as being bought either. More than likely they were stolen and never reported missing. Whoever did this, they more than likely killed the chemist after he did it for them."

"No witnesses." She nodded as she paced the kitchen. Her body moved like she'd invented movement. Slim and muscled, he could see that she was comfortable with herself. But he also knew that if she needed to, and he'd seen it first hand, she could be as lethal as his cat when pissed off with just that same sexy body. And her clothing fit her like it had been painted on her.

He'd noticed her clothing when he'd been looking for something to pull on earlier. Not that he thought any of her things would fit him. She was smaller by a great deal, but he'd noticed that her closet was mostly empty except for a large gun safe, and there wasn't a single dress in the big area. Mostly there were T-shirts, black, as well as a few pair of cargo pants, also black. He'd gone snooping to see what else she might have hidden. There wasn't a great deal of either personal items or dressy clothing. All he'd been able to find was more guns than he'd thought were in all of the state.

"What are you cooking?" He told her cookies and steak. "You have to tell me how you came up with that combo.

Potatoes and steak, yeah, I get that, but not cookies. And I didn't think you could eat chocolate."

"Canines can't eat chocolate. Cats can, I guess. At least *we* can. This is my mom's recipe." He handed her a hot cookie as soon as he pulled the pan from the oven. "So, are we not going to talk about you being my mate?"

"Not yet. I have to not think about things for a minute to clear out the cobwebs. Tell me why you had your brother run a test on me being sick. I'm assuming that's where he got his information." Colin told her that it had been Boyd's idea, not his. "So he's the smarter one of the two of you? Perhaps he needs a mate too."

He growled low and told her that it didn't work that way. But she was off on another line of questions before he could explain it to her. If he even had to.

"I'm not going to be going back into active duty, or so they're telling me. I can have a desk job and recruit some shit heads, but they won't let me go back to what I was doing. Did you know that?" He told her that he did, Tony had told him. "I'm not sure what to do with myself right now. I don't know how to do anything but give orders and expect people to obey them. But I have some metal in my body that's keeping me from what I need to do. Or so they told me."

"I'm guessing from that you don't believe that part either. May I make a suggestion?" She said sure but not to expect miracles from it. "I was thinking that the person that didn't tell you what was really in those drugs might have been the same one that told you you're not fit for active duty. My brother Boyd can run some tests and see.... Where are you going?"

"I have a phone around here somewhere. I was going to call him and see when I can come in." He pulled the last of the cookies out of the oven and went to find her. She was in her office on the phone, and he sat down while she finished her conversation. When she hung up, he knew that Boyd was going to help her. "I have to go in sometime when the office is closed. I don't need to alert whoever is doing this to me that I'm...we're onto them."

"Good idea. And Boyd is the best at what he does." She nodded and told him she knew. "You do? And when did you find this out?"

"I knew your brother Hawkins before he joined up. Not long before, but enough that I had him and all of you investigated. I wanted him on my team. But I also didn't want some looney there either. So I checked him out." He waited for her to explain, or at the very least tell him what she'd found out. "Hawkins proved himself even before the reports came back about you guys. He has been at my side since the beginning. Hawkins is one of the best soldiers I know. He's the type of man that you know when he says that he has your back, you can damned well bet he has it."

"He has a great deal of respect for you as well." Lauren said nothing as she sat here. The big desk was still in some sort of wrapping, and the chair that more than likely came with it was sitting by the couch. She was currently sitting in the wingback that he was sure was supposed to be in front of the fireplace. The place, the entire house for that matter, had an open freedom feeling to it. "You designed this place, didn't you?"

There was an openness that he wouldn't have thought would work in this room and the others on this main floor. Doorways were wide, with pocket doors that slid silently into their places. The furniture was new but had a worn, comfortable look to it, and the shelves—and this room had plenty—were filled with books. No foo-foo, as his mom called it. Just books.

"There were three rooms in the house that I spent the first years of my life in. My room, my biological parents' room, and a central room that I'm sure was supposed to be a living room. There was no electric to the place, no phone, and while there was running water, the toilet had to be flushed by dumping a five gallon bucket of water into it and then rinsed out with the hose that also doubled as a shower for me. I never saw my parents use it. Though after some thought, I suppose they did occasionally." She stared off into the room, completely forgetting about him, he was sure. "Neither of them worked. Only at trying to kill each other. And me when they saw me. I tried my best to stay out of their sights as much as I could. Food was a luxury for me. I'd hoard it when there was any, which was usually taken from a dumpster somewhere. Or if the school would have enough for there to be leftovers, I'd wrap it up in newspaper that was in abundance at the house and take it. That didn't happen often, but I would save it."

"Is that why the pantry is so stocked and you have two deep freezers that have more food in it than most small stores do?" She said it was. "And this house. You built large because of what you didn't have."

"I used my first bonus check to purchase the land that I grew up on. My intentions were to let it go, let trees take it over so that I'd never have to think of this place again. But then Mom told me that it was unhealthy, that I should make it something else. Something pretty. So with my next two checks, I used the money to put this here. It's been a long process, but I love the results. It's the only place I call home anymore. My parents, Peter and Mary, have always welcomed me there, of course, but this is where I can be whatever I want. Which is usually not a killer."

He loved the house as well and told her that. "You thought I was Pete the other day. You thanked him for watching over the place. Does he know why you did this? Any of the other Burchers?"

"Oh yes. He knows. I have never...not many people know, but he was my little brother and I told him." He heard the timer go off in the kitchen to let him know the potatoes were close enough that he had to put on the vegetables. "Colin, I don't want you to be killed because of me."

"I don't want that either." He stood up and told her to come with him. "We'll figure this out. Once we do then the rest should be easy. I'm not saying that it won't be difficult, but we can figure this out."

At least he hoped so. He didn't want to lose her by her getting hurt, or him either. As he began listing the veggies that he'd unearthed in the larger freezer, Colin came to a realization that nearly took him to his knees. He was in love with his mate.

Chapter 6

Rich watched his sons. All of them were about as big as a house, yet as gentle as kittens around the young woman. Even Dustin, his baby, seemed to be in awe of Lauren, and really, Rich didn't blame him. He was sorta in love with her himself. He glanced over at his own mate and she smiled at him.

"She's got them eating out of her hands, and she doesn't have a clue what to do with them. Just look at her. She's about ready to bash in a couple of heads. And if Dustin calls her 'Miss' again, I think he'll be the first to go." Rich laughed and saw the moment that Dustin realized he was in big trouble. "Here it comes."

"If you call me that one more time, even if you mean to call me Miss Lauren, I'm going to take your dick off and sew it to your forehead so there will be little doubt that you're a dick head." Dustin grinned at Lauren and she continued. "You think I'm kidding, then you're going to look pretty fucking stupid the next time some girl wants you to date her."

The look on Dustin's face was priceless. But when he reached up and rubbed his forehead, as if expecting his dick to be right there, Rich lost control of his laughter. Bea only cleared her throat and order was resumed, but he still chuckled whenever he thought of it, or only had to look at his son's face.

Colin was a changed man. Not only did he seem more relaxed than he'd seen him in a very long time, but Rich could see that he was happy, and a little in awe himself of his new mate. Small wonder, the girl could do and had more than likely done just about everything there was, and tomorrow she was gonna teach Bea and a couple of the boys how to fire a weapon, with Hawkins's help. He wasn't really sure about it yet. He wanted them safe, yes, but a gun in the house was dangerous. Even if you could use it well.

He glanced at his second oldest. Hawkins had always been the one who liked it organized. If it could be put in a box, labeled, and put on a shelf, he'd have it done. His room, even when he shared one with his brothers, was neat, tidy, and things in order. Tallest to smallest, colors together, and even his pictures were in order of year taken. It had driven Rich nuts whenever he had to take him to the store for something. The cart would resemble one of them games where each piece would fit perfectly against the other before it disappeared. Never had a cashier that wouldn't remark on it either. And right now, he seemed lost.

He'd talked to his boy a lot since he'd been home. Being on medical, as he'd called it, had given him a bit more time here than had been originally planned. But he was thinking that Hawkins, like Lauren, was ready to skedaddle now. They'd visited and healed well enough, and now they felt the need to go. He wondered how Colin was gonna take it when his mate left without telling him where she was. Not well, he'd imagine.

Boyd came into the living room just then, and he gave them all a hug. Rich sure was glad that his boys hadn't outgrown the need to hug him. It made his whole day just to have some big arms wrap around him tightly. As Boyd kissed his mom on her cheek, he looked around. Rich wondered what sort of things he'd been able to find out about Lauren.

Just this morning he'd been in town when he'd seen Lauren coming out of Boyd's office. She told him that they were running tests to see what sort of damage had been done to her. Colin had been called away then. He hated it, so Rich had volunteered to go to the mall with the woman, something he would have normally avoided like it was contagious. But she was a pretty young thing and he wanted to show off. But mostly what they did was walk the big area, not even going into the shops, which suited him just fine. Her too, he guessed. Then she sort of spoke up, like she needed to talk or bust. He was just fine to listen to her too.

"They've been lying to me." He asked her if she really hadn't been expecting that, they were the government after all. "No. I mean I suppose I should have expected it, but now I'm worried about a great many things that I hadn't thought of before. Like, why would they kill off innocent men when all they really wanted dead was me?"

Rich didn't have an answer for her and waited while she went to try on some jeans. He did wonder for a minute if she knew she was buying them in the men's section, then looked at the selection in the women's department. He didn't think his own wife would wear any of those things. They were so spangled up, he thought they'd look like some sort of seventies big ball on a dance floor. When she came out, he noticed that she was limping again. Rich had asked her if she was all right.

"Yeah, I guess. Sometimes there is this pain in my knee that really bothers me if I twist it up funny. Pulling on pants in a cardboard box isn't really ideal for changing for me." She grinned at him. "I've been around men most of my life. I was tempted to come out of it and just try them on where there was more room. But I figured they'd toss us out on our asses, and I'd have my naked ass hanging out when we headed for the car."

Yeah, Rich thought, he did love that girl. She told it like it was, said it like she meant it, and even put enough color in it for you that you had to just smile. He wanted so badly to be a part of the meeting that was going on right now that Boyd had taken her and Colin into the office for.

"You suppose they found something that didn't ring true with what that doctor said to her?" He'd bet money on it and said that to Bea. "I think you might be right. That poor girl. Doing all this for our country to have someone try and hurt her. Makes me want to go out there and do him some harm and see how he likes it."

He stared at his wife of nearly fifty years, then laughed. "I think that our Lauren is rubbing off on you. Whatever has gotten into you lately?"

"Meanness I guess." Bea leaned her head on his shoulder. "You think that when things settle, they'll have some children? I've been waiting on a grandchild for so long that I feel like it's never going to happen. And Rich, I can't help but think that any children those two have will be hellions. More so than we might be able to handle if they let us sit them. Don't you think?"

"I think they'll have us some. They might be a bit on the ornery side, but I think they'll be fine. Like their mother, I'm hoping with a little of Colin sprinkled in for good measure. Can you imagine him when there is a little girl around?" Rich had wanted a little girl so badly that he could have tasted it. He loved his sons, but one of them had better have him a granddaughter. He needed one. "She'll be the apple of her uncles' eyes too. Any of them would be. Boy or girl."

"I'd like a granddaughter too after so many sons. They could all have them for all I care. Little girls are so adorable. But I think you might be right on them being a little like their mom. She'd have some tough girls and tougher boys." He thought so too, and tried to imagine what one would look like.

The door opened to the office, and he could see that things had gone just as they'd thought. The reports were wrong. Rich wanted to go and hug them both, but he was sort of afraid. Not of them but for them. They were being lied to, and someone was going to have to pay for that.

Rich started to ask and saw Lauren shake her head. His mouth snapped closed with an audible sound, and he watched as she walked to the door and let in two men. Both of them looked like they meant business, and no one moved as they walked around the room with big wands, going over each and every thing in the room.

His house, apparently, had been bugged. After the men adjusted them all—twenty-three, as it turned out in this room alone—Lauren and Colin sat down with Boyd and told them what they'd found.

"I have a chip in my body that turns these recording devices on as soon as I enter the room. These men are going to go through the rest of the house and see about marking them. When I leave, they'll turn them back on, but I won't return here until we figure this out." Bea said she didn't want them there. "If we remove them, they'll know I'm on to their shit. Right now they're only going to think there is a glitch that turned these off. If they know that we're aware of them, there is no telling what they'll do."

Rich had a feeling she knew just what they'd do but was sparing them. He looked around his room that now felt dirty. He wanted to go and take them out, toss them away, and never worry about people listening in on his conversation again. But he could also see the point that Lauren was making. They needed the extra time, she'd told them, to get to the person in charge.

"Do you know who it is?" She didn't say anything to his question. "You might not know, but you have an idea, don't you?"

"Yes. And one that, if I'm wrong, will most definitely get me killed." Several names popped into his head and he had to lean back or get dizzy. The names that he thought of were...well, she'd be right about getting killed. Any or all of them were high up on the list of just plain scary people. "I'm going to go home now. I have to...my house is clean, or it was when I left. I need to take care of a couple of things there too. Remember, when I'm gone, the recorders don't work, so you won't have to hide what you say here. And once a week, these guys, and only these guys, will be around to look and make sure that there is nothing else added to your house. Be careful of who you invite in to do work, too. Don't trust anyone unless you ask me first."

When she stood up, Colin did as well. If Rich was honest with himself, he'd like to tell his son to stay there where he could protect him. But he knew, deep in his heart, that Lauren could do a better job of keeping them both safe than he could. As soon as they left, the two men came back in and worked at the little devices, and Rich went out on the deck. They were no longer being listened to, but he didn't want to be in his house anymore.

~~~

The sweep of her home took less than two hours. No devices were found in the home, but there were several on the outside. They'd know her every entrance and exit, but not what she did or said inside. Colin came into the kitchen where she was and sat at the table with her.

"Who?" She only shook her head. To say it aloud made it seem more real. And that was something she didn't want to think about. "Okay, so do you know why this person or persons are doing this? Because I'm betting it has nothing to do with you being a female."

"I don't think so either, but I don't really know. I have to talk to Hawkins. I mean, he might not know either, but he might have a better picture on this than I have at the moment. All I can think of right now is that chip and that I was lied to. By a lot of people who I should have been able to trust." Boyd had not only told her that she didn't have any shrapnel in her, but that she had two small chips. One on her knee and the other at the base of her spine. The scar had been hidden by the wounds she'd gotten.

"The one that tells them where you are, what are you going to do about that? I know you wanted Boyd to take it out, but then what? Won't the same thing happen as the recorders at my parents' house?" She got up and poured some tea in two glasses and got the leftover cookies from yesterday. He'd noticed that she rarely ate sweets, turning them down for fruit when she could get it, but right now he thought she was getting them out for him. "Lauren, we'll get this worked out."

"I know." She took one of the cookies out of the plastic container and held it in her hands as she sat there. "I'm going to have you remove the tracker if you can. If not, then I'll find someone else. I don't want to involve your brothers any more than we have too. Hawkins is already involved, but he has an advantage over the rest of them in that he can use a weapon and use it well."

"I can see that." He took the cookie from her when she started crumbling it up and handed her a branch of grapes. She ate two of the small green orbs while he got up and took some fish he'd been marinating from the fridge. "Then what happens to it?"

"I stick it to something that I want them to follow that's not me when I have to be where I don't want them." He wasn't sure he liked the sound of that. "Or, and this is more than likely a better idea, I remove it, but keep it on my person until I can't take them with me. Like on a mission to figure this out. In the meantime, I have it in my pocket, so I have some control over it. But, Colin, you can't be with me when I go out. I have to make sure that you're safe."

He'd already figured that part out as well. When she went out, and she would have to, it would be without him. He didn't know anything about guns, less about being covert, and he would get them both killed if he even tried to help her on this. She knew things and she knew people who knew more than he ever would that could get her help. He would be a burden. It was hard to swallow, but he knew his own limitations when this shit was involved.

"I need to do something. I can't just be one of those people that sit around waiting for the call. You know what I mean." She nodded but didn't look at him. "Lauren, this person or persons you think this is, is it bad?"

"The worst." She got up then and tossed away the empty branch of grapes. He held her when she curled her arms around his waist from behind, and stood still while she leaned against him. It was all he could do not to beg her not to leave him. But they wouldn't have a normal life with this hanging over their heads.

"Don't trust anyone with any information. Your family will be fine, but no one else. Not Tony, the doctors, or even the people that you've worked with for years. Everyone can be bought, and when they can't be, there are those that will prey on them until they roll over to do what they need. I'm not saying that Tony is involved, but he may be chipped as well, and we can't take the chance that he is." He nodded, afraid for them. "Victoria is coming here as soon as it's twilight. When she gets here, I'd like for you to give her a taste of your blood. I trust her with my life and yours too."

"All right." He turned then and held her. "I'd like for you to do the same with my family. They have your scent now, but your blood will make it so that you can talk to them if you need them."

He noticed that she didn't mention her family, and he also realized that they had been pretty absent from their lives until now. He started to ask her about it, if they were part of who she thought was doing this, but she spoke first.

"My mom and dad don't want to be involved, or they'd like not to be involved in what's going on. They...it's because of Pete. They're afraid that he'll get hurt too. I don't blame them. I've tried my best to keep him out of my life, but he's been there all along. I don't think they realize how much...we talked all the time when I had service, and he'd keep me up on what was going on at home." She tightened her hold on him. "Pete isn't involved, none of them are, but they worry about him."

"I'll see about sending over some people to keep an eye on them for you." She told him she'd taken care of it. And when he thought about it, he thought she'd be better equipped to know who to trust than him. "Anything I can do to help out with this?"

"Yes." She looked up at him. "I have given this a great deal of thought. And I want you to convert me. I know that it's hard and that it'll put me out for a while, but I'll be able to do so much more than just get beat to shit. I'll be able to run with you."

"All right." He lifted her chin up more and kissed her. She tasted of grapes and chocolate, his mate and love. When he deepened the kiss, he thought of all the things he wanted to do to her and lifted her up, cradling her body around his. "I need you."

Her clothing was shreds by the time he got her naked. Her panties had been small pieces of silk at one point and not just threads on the floor. Her jeans—new, she'd told him—didn't survive either. The zipper had burst the moment he'd tried to pull her pants off without undoing it.

His pants were down around his thighs when he slammed into her. She held him, tearing at his shirt, which he'd not bothered to remove, until he was bare chested. The moment she moved her mouth to his nipple and bit down, Colin wanted it rough. And he was pretty sure she did as well. Pulling from her heat, he pulled her off the counter and turned her around.

"Hold on." He wasn't sure that she understood him. His voice had deepened with his need, but the moment he slammed his cock into her pussy from behind, she cried out that she was coming. Colin leaned her over the counter and, holding her head tightly to it, he fucked her like the animal that he was, and then leaned over and bit hard into her shoulder. He knew that his cat was ready to take her as well.

When she came the second then third time, screaming out his name as she did so, he picked her up and took her to their bedroom. As soon as she was on the bed, he let his cat take him.

He wants you. Nodding, she sat on the edge and held onto the mattress while he moved toward her. *Let him taste you, Lauren. Then we'll start the process now. He wants you to be his mate fully.*

"Please hurry. I'm so close to coming now thinking about his tongue on me."

He lapped at her pussy, then at her thigh. Lauren curled her fingers into his fur at his head and opened her legs wider for him. His cat leapt to her and licked her from gate to clit, then nipped at her.

Lauren screamed. Her body fell back against the mattress while his cat feasted on her. Every time she came, crying out when she did, his cat would growl low, drinking her cream down as fast as she released it. When he nudged at her thigh again, he knew he was going to bite her, and Lauren did as well. At her command to do it, his cat bit down onto her creamy thigh and Colin heard bones break.

The process. He knew some of what had to be done but not all. Colin also knew that there was going to be a great deal of pain for her. His cat never wavered in his duty to his mate.

The next bite was at her other leg, this time at her calf. Colin had never done this before, converted anyone, but he knew his cat would know just how to do it. When Lauren whimpered slightly, holding him to her body, Colin told her he was sorry.

"Don't be. I need this as much as you do." He moved up her body, telling his cat to be gentler to her. And when he licked her face, they both tasted the tears. "I'm not going to lie to you, it hurts like a motherfucker, but I'll be all right. Just tell him to get it done so we can move on with our lives."

He hoped so because his cat licked her belly then, and Colin was worried that this would bring him to his knees should she scream out in pain. As soon as he sank his teeth into her, Colin felt her pain. And when she went limp, her hand sliding from his cat's head to the bed, he knew that he'd either killed her or she'd passed out. Christ, this was the scariest thing he'd ever done in all his life.

It was another twenty minutes of his cat holding her in the belly before he tasted the difference. His cat must have as well, because soon after, he let her go, then let Colin take him back. Picking her up, he laid her on the other side of the bed and stripped the sheets off and cleaned her up. The amount of blood wasn't as bad as he'd thought it would be, but it was still enough to make him slightly nervous.

When the bed was remade and Lauren was cleaned up, he sat in the chair next to her. Colin thought about getting into the big bed with her but wanted her to rest, knowing that she needed that more than him being close to her. It was well after midnight when he felt Boyd touch his mind.

I found a number on that tracer that she has in her body. He asked him what that meant. *It means that I can give this to someone and they can find the manufacturer for her. I tried to call you guys. Is the phone out?*

It's in the kitchen and she's...I changed her tonight. Boyd said nothing for a long time, and Colin felt the need to explain. *She's hoping this will give her an edge that she didn't have. I agree with her. And she wants to be able to run with me.*

Yeah, I can see that. And understand why she'd want this edge, but it seems to me that she's going to be under for a while and I worry for you and her. She's one hell of a woman. Colin laughed and said he agreed. Then he remembered what she'd told him about trusting anyone. He told Boyd to pass it on to the others too.

Hawkins already let us know some of that. He also told me to not put these records in my office or home. I gave them to him and he said he knew just where to hide them. Colin wondered why they thought having them around was dangerous, then remembered the surveillance cameras everywhere. *Colin, did she tell you who she might think is out to get her and Hawkins?*

No. She said it was bad and I let it go. I think she's still trying to wrap her mind around it. I think they fucked with Larson's account too. He said that someone had a freeze on his checking account and he wasn't able to buy food. Lauren gave him all the cash she had, and he was pretty upset but not at her. You heard anything from the rest of the family about that?

That might explain why I couldn't pay my monthly dues this morning. The bank said that there was a strange hold on my account when I inquired about it, and then a couple of hours later, they called to say it was gone. I don't know. Are they fucking with our livelihood because of Lauren and Hawkins? Colin said he didn't know but would ask Lauren when she woke up. *I'll come by in a couple of days to check on her. I'm sure she'll be fine, but I want to make sure that she's doing well anyway. I love her, by the way. Have you told her that you love her yet?*

I only just figured it out myself. And not yet. I was waiting for her to settle down a little. She scares the shit out of me if you want to know the truth. Boyd said she did him too, a little. *I've never…having a mate changes things, you know? Like your entire outlook on life is different.*

I'm sure it does. And hopefully someone will come along and change all of us for the good. Or be willing to bash our heads in so that we get it. They both laughed. *Take care of her for us, Colin. And let her take care of you when she's up and around.*

Colin said that he would, on both accounts. When Boyd told him he'd get back to him in the morning, Colin got up and moved to the door that led out onto a private deck. He loved this place, and all the property around it. Going to the main part of the house to lock up and make sure the oven was off, he saw two wolves on the front decking that surrounded that part of the house, and then a bear, big as a fucking car, sitting by the back door. He knew that they were there for her, at her request, and that made him feel a great deal better. She really did have people she trusted, he thought, as he locked up and headed back to the office to use the computer.

Colin knew it was going to be a long few days until she woke up. And in the meantime, he was going to see about moving his things here too. She'd already told him to, and he figured he'd get some work done while she rested.

Victoria showed up in the living room just as he was going through there.

Chapter 7

Tony sat down hard. He wasn't sure what to think right now, only that this was going to get him in deep shit. He looked at the report in front of him again, this time trying not to focus so much on the ages of the dead but the names there and where they had worked. All the dead and their ranks with ages were of the people killed in the ambush of Lauren and Hawkins. But the real kicker was that all of them were from the United States and serving under him in some capacity. The men that served their country were getting younger and younger all the time. And dying for no other reason than greed and stupidity.

The report had been given to him by Lauren earlier that morning without a word spoken between them. It had been a chance meeting, her bumping into him as she walked by him. It took him several seconds to realize that she'd given him something. And now he had information that he was sure he wasn't supposed to ever see.

"Sir?" He looked up at his assistant, Private Mark Wayne, and smiled. He wasn't sure that it looked good or not, but the man smiled back. "I thought I heard you say my name. I've been working on the computers for over an hour now."

"What's wrong with them now?" Mark told him they'd been running slowly since the department came in and did some upgrades on them. Tony glanced down at the report and the names on it and his mind went into overdrive. More puzzle pieces were falling into place all around him. "When was that?"

"Last week. Oh, that's right, you were out with the emergency. Yes, sir. They came in saying that all the computers needed to be upgraded. Then they said that the phones needed to be replaced as well. If you ask me, they look just like they did before, but I'm not a computer whiz like some are." Neither was he, but Tony would bet his last dollar that nothing more than a bug had been in the "upgrade" to the computers. "I'm ready to call the computer help desk. I'll be right here if you need me, sir."

Tony waved him off and said nothing. He eyed the computer, then the phone. He wasn't going to be using them for anything important from now on. And on his way home, he was picking up a burner phone, one that only he had the number for. Christ, he thought of Lauren and Hawkins. How to contact them?

He was sure that they knew. Even if they didn't, Tony had a feeling that they would go to other means to contact him if they needed him. He did have a sudden thought, one that frightened him a little. He didn't want them to think he had anything to do with this. But then he realized she would never have given him what she had if she suspected him of anything.

"Hello." The beautiful woman standing at his desk nearly had him reaching for his sidearm. But she smiled at him and told him it would do him no good. "I'm not there, you see. Or here—however you wish to see it. But I would prefer that you not speak. That young man out there is stupid, but he can hear quite well for a human. If you could just…I don't know, nod when you think it's necessary, and shake that lovely head of yours when you don't."

He wasn't sure how to ask her anything, but she seemed to understand his unspoken questions. "Lauren sent me. She said that you need to purchase yourself a pick and go-phone soon. In the meantime, she has me coming back and forth. Oh, and soon I should like to taste you. Not sexually, though had she told me you were so yummy looking, I might have insisted on that as well." He cleared his throat, never having been this embarrassed before. "Anyway. She said that you have more than likely been bugged. Not just here, but at your home as well as your cars. And Lauren said that you should learn to walk more. It's better for your health. And that the park where she showed you how she was capable of caring for herself has a nice bench too."

Tony nodded. He knew that place, and he picked up his coat to go there now. But before he could leave the room, his boss, Brigadier General Garth Wilson, moved into his office like he owned it. Victoria smiled at him and told him to pay attention to the man, there would be questions for him later.

"I just got off the phone with the president. He is not a happy man." Victoria said that he wasn't, but not for the reasons he was about to hear. "He is trying his best to get in touch with Burcher and she's not cooperating. He wanted me to tell you to get her ass in here pronto. And that man of hers too, McCullough."

He means Hawkins, not Colin. They are unaware of him as yet being her mate. Tell him that she's been ill, her wounds are bothering her. Tony told him what she said. *Very good. Now, as in an offhanded thought, tell him that you thought she was going to the company doctor today. That you think she's not as well as she had you believe.* Tony relayed the messages, even going so far as to tell the man that he was avoiding her in the event she had some sort of flu.

"Good. Good. He can fix her right up. I have a feeling that woman is not following protocol and is fucking with the system. You know how much I hate when she does that. But you don't have to worry about catching anything from her. I'm sure it's just her wounds acting up. They'll fix her right up if she'd just do as she was told."

Tony did know how much Garth hated Lauren. He had since the very beginning of her career. He glanced at Victoria when she told him what to say next.

"Hawkins hasn't been healing as well either. I heard from his family that they might have to amputate his arm, poor boy, and after all that he's done for us. Did you know it was that bad?" Tony was watching Wilson's face or he might have missed the look of joy there. When Victoria spoke this time, he had a feeling that she was talking to Lauren even as she spoke to him.

He wants them both dead for some reason. And having them go to the doctor is where Lauren thinks something is going to happen. I'm to tell you that they have no intentions of going to him, but she wanted you to see his reaction. This man is not to be trusted. Tony said no shit before he could think that they weren't alone.

"What was that? What did you say?" He asked Wilson what he meant and tried his best to keep his face from giving him away. "I thought you said something. Never mind. As I was saying, the president needs to talk to the two of them. Might be an honor or something in this for them. You do know that the president, he thinks the world of that woman."

That woman. He'd called her that twice now. And when Tony looked at Victoria again, he knew that she had some information that he needed. Or that he wanted. Either way, he had to speak to her alone. And he thought the park would be the best place for it.

"I was just stepping out. I thought about heading for the park to run a few miles, clear my head. Did you want to join me?" He knew that Wilson would never run anywhere unless it was for food. The man had to weigh at the very least three hundred pounds, and he had several chins to show for it. "I'm sure I can find you some running clothes if you want to."

"No, no. You go right ahead. I have things to see to here. You said she was going to the company doctor today, didn't you?" He said that he'd confirm it but was sure that's what she'd said. "Good. Okay, I have some calls to make. I'll speak to you later. Good work on this. Very good work."

Lauren is in the park waiting for you, Victoria told him when they entered the elevator. *She said that if you had a tail, which I'm to understand she thinks you have now, then you are to go to the bench and wait for her signal. And before you ask, no, I have no idea what it might be. Very cloak and dagger, isn't it?*

It was scary was what it was. As he made his way to the park, his shoes and a T-shirt stuffed in his duffle, he thought about all the shit that had gone down in the last few weeks. Well, month he supposed now. Since the week before Lauren and Hawkins had been hurt and her team taken out.

Changing in the small room, he was a little disconcerted to have Victoria in the outer room waiting on him. He was sure that she was enjoying his discomfort much more than he thought she should, so when he came out, dressed, she looked him up and down, and he felt his cock stretch in his shorts. Christ, he needed to find a woman if an image of a vampire, albeit a beautiful one, was doing this to him.

You should come to my home tonight. We could have a very good time. I can show you things that you have never dreamed up. He only finished tying his shoes as she continued. *Do you like it hard and fast, Anthony? I do. And if you tied me to the bed while you fucked me, I'd really make it worth your while.*

He was rock hard when he left the changing area and headed to the toilets. Her soft laughter accompanied him into the stall, where he tried to reason with his cock that right now was not the time for him to be stone hard. When she appeared in the little stall with him, Tony realized that she was really there this time as soon as he felt her breath on his cheek.

"Let me help you." He wanted to tell her no, that he had it under control, but she reached into his gym pants and wrapped her hand around him. "So thick. I bet you give as good as you get, don't you? I'd like nothing more than to feel you giving it to me, Anthony. Hard and brutal. I bet you could make me like it gentle too, couldn't you?"

"I have to meet Lauren."

Victoria slid to her knees in front of him and took him deep into her mouth even as she pulled his pants down to his ankles. Christ, he nearly came when she cupped his now bare balls in her hand and sucked him hard. Fucking her talented mouth, all he could think about was coming down her throat. But the thought of fucking her right there in the stall had him jerking her up from him and picking her up.

"Strip." She was naked before he finished the word. And when she lifted up her heavy breast and offered it to him, Tony took the morsel into his mouth as he turned them toward the door and entered her, lifting her small body up and her pussy right where he needed it. "Fuck, yes."

She was tight, wet, and hot. He wanted it to last. Fucking this woman would be an experience that he'd never soon forget. She wrapped her ankles around his hips and held him to her as he pounded her.

"Come in me. Please, come in me, Anthony. I want to drink from you when you do." He felt his balls tighten and his body tense for release. Make it last, he told himself, make it go on forever. But the moment she dug her nails into his back and cried out her release, he exploded inside of her. Then she pulled his throat to her mouth and bit him.

Nothing could have prepared him for the sensation of coming this way. Victoria wrapped around him, his throat being abused as his cock filled twice more and released inside of her. His body didn't just release, he realized as he rested his head against her breast, but detonated several times in a matter of minutes. He wondered briefly if he'd survive a bedroom with her.

"Oh, honey. Oh, my dear boy. That was fucking fantastic." He lifted his head up, not sure he could do much more than that, and looked at her. "Please tell me that you're going home with me tonight. I'm sure that you can top this."

"I think you killed me just now." Her laughter rang around him and he smiled. "I have to go and see Lauren. I'm sure she's worried about me."

"She trusts you, and I'll tell her that you were...delayed." He didn't even want to think what she might tell her. "She's going to smell me on you. I think she might be...well, happy for us both. I know that I am. Lauren has been telling me for years that I should hook up with you. I'm glad that I got the chance today."

"Will you be all right? I know it's still pretty light out." She told him she would go straight home and to bed. "If I can, I would like to see you again. Not just for sex, though that was wonderful, but Lauren told me you play chess."

"I do. And it's a date." As clothing appeared on her, he pulled his own clothing back to rights. He was as relaxed as he'd ever been, and she laughed when he leaned against the wall again. "I can't wait until tonight then. We'll play come chess. Then you can fuck me all night, taking us both to highs we've never been to before. Take care, and tell Lauren that she was right about you. You are one of the good guys."

Tony left the stall and noticed that there were several men in the room with him. When none of them said anything about what they might have heard, he washed his face and hands and made his way out. Talking to Lauren was going to give him so much, he just knew it. But Christ almighty, he hadn't felt this good in decades.

~~~

It had taken a little time getting used to being able to hear everything. She looked at the man and woman jogging toward her, and heard him telling the woman that he was worried that his wife was catching onto their affair. The second man was singing softly. The head jacks in his ears were blasting music to his head, and Lauren wondered if he had a hearing problem. Plus, he was singing the wrong words to a very popular song. And off key.

She saw Tony as he jogged toward her, or at least the bench she was near. There wasn't any way that he'd know it was her unless she let him because of the costume she had on; a dress of Bea's, a hat that belonged to a long dead aunt, and shoes that made her feet look ten feet long. When he sat down, testing his pulse at his throat, she noticed the bite mark and laughed. He glanced at her, then did a double take. She guessed that he could smell it was her before he could recognize her.

"You're a cat now, congratulations." She smiled at him, sat down beside him, and opened her purse that had all the things in it he'd need. "Victoria said that you needed to talk to me. Are you all right?"

"Yes. I have a phone for you to use. And the numbers are all programed in it. Mine now, as well as Hawkins's and Colin's. Don't call him unless you have to." He leaned over and retied his shoes while she continued. "I think Wilson is in on this. So is the president."

Tony snapped his shoelace in half, and she had to laugh. When he looked at her, she nodded once as he leaned back. She was as sure as shit that they were both doing this, but how to prove it was going to be tricky.

"Now what happens? Do we blow this out of the water or do you have a plan?" She told him she did, but stood up and dumped her purse out. He bent to pick her things up when she did, and she stuffed a thumb drive in his sock and handed him an earpiece as well as the burner phone.

"Hawkins is coming. Put in the earpiece and listen to what he has to say." As she walked away, she watched as Hawkins came toward her. As he passed her, she knew that he was going to be all right; she just hoped that Tony would be. He was about to be told things that would not be easy to take. Or maybe they would be. He had more than likely already read the file she'd passed to him this morning.

Lauren watched the area so that neither man was followed. She'd seen the two men that had come in with Tony peel off when he started to run. That was the nice thing about this area. If you didn't jog or roller blade, you stuck out like a sore thumb. She knew the exact moment that Hawkins told Tony a little of what they'd found out. His small stumble might have been funny had it not been so scary.

The president. *Who would have thought it?* she wondered. He'd been a good man on the surface, they'd found out. There wasn't a time when he'd been in trouble that anyone could pinpoint on him. Some even thought he was a loving and kind husband and father. But all of that, every part of the man's life, had been a well-fabricated lie, and had been helped to be perfect by the one person she would never have pegged as a traitor to his country.

President Joe Irwin and his sidekick, Brigadier General Garth Wilson, were in together so deep she wondered who was the first to approach the other in this thing. And the reason she was being targeted—she and Hawkins—was because they'd been in the White House a little too early and had thwarted Joe's plans to have his wife and son killed for the sympathy vote this coming election.

Sex and war never are far apart. She smiled at the voice in her head. Victoria had been a great deal of help this time, and Lauren was going to thank her again when she saw her in person. *That man, the one you had me go see, he's not married or anything, is he? I just had the most cardinal sin good time with him if he is.*

No. He's widowed, but I don't think they were very happy together anyway. She never understood his need to be in the service, and he couldn't understand her need to fuck whoever she could while he was gone. I think she died in the arms of a lover when his wife found out about them. And please don't tell me any details. Victoria laughed. *He's a good man. And one that is going to need someone when this is over. He's going to take a lot of heat from the press when this falls out.*

He's my mate. Lauren said nothing. She was thrilled to death for them both, but she also knew that Tony had told her that he'd never love again. *I haven't told him as yet. I might not. You know that of late I've had the feeling that I've had enough of this world. Ending my life at this moment in time would not be that bad. I found him. If he rejects me then there is nothing lost.*

For him there would be. Victoria told her that he'd never know. *I think he would, if he doesn't already. His cat, his tiger, he would have recognized you, right?*

I suppose. But I think he was so...grateful for my assistance that he forgot that part. I know I sort of did when he became so...manly with me. Lauren laughed. *Well, you did tell me that you wanted no details. He is a hell of a man. Seen to me before he —*

Enough. Victoria laughed again. *When you went to see him, what did he say? I'm assuming because he's here that he took it all right?*

He had something on his desk when I arrived, and I'm betting it's the stuff you said you were going to share with him. Then a man, dressed in more medals than he had brains — Wilson, his badge said — came in and spoke to him. I could read his mind. He is not a good man. Lauren told her that he wasn't. *The phones in Tony's office have been tapped. Computers are shadowed. I know the meaning of that now, so that's not a good thing either. This Wilson person, he was there to make sure that Tony didn't figure it out. I guess the computers were acting up and he wanted to make sure that the guy out front called the right people, and Tony was in his office when this Wilson person did it. I think Tony knows that he's being watched there as well.*

It's why we met him here. I'm sure that his office at home is monitored as well. They want to keep him out of the loop, and in order to do that, they have to make sure that he doesn't figure shit out. Why is the question. Other than him telling on them, what else could there be? I think they're going to dump this in his lap and stand by while he takes the fall. It's what I would do if I was that much of a shithead. Victoria asked if she wanted her to go and see his home. *That would be great. I was trying to figure out how to send someone there without alerting them about it. You know what to look for, right? The hum should alert you as to where they will be.*

I'll go now. I can keep in the shadows of his home and see what I can find. We're having dinner tonight and playing some chess, as well as other things. Lauren said she didn't want to know. *I'll let you know about the other though. As soon as I know, you will.*

When her connection closed, Lauren moved toward the bench where she'd been sitting waiting on Tony. He was going to be hurt by this. He had a great deal of respect for the office of presidency, not to mention the man was true blue all the way through his body. But things had to be put out in the open. Otherwise more people would be hurt and things would fall apart more than they were now.

"How did it go?" Colin sat beside her and leaned back on the bench. She was still dressed as an older women, and she nearly laughed out loud when she glanced over at him. He was dressed similarly, but as a man not a female. "Hawkins said that he didn't think anyone recognized you, by the way. He said that he almost didn't."

"No, I don't think so either. But Tony is pretty upset. He's going to be more so when he gets finished talking with your brother." She stood up and moved slowly. "Would you take an old woman to lunch?"

"I would love to. I have to go by my office in a little while. There are a few matters I have to look into that I sort of have been putting off. I'm sure that you have things to do as well." She told him that she did. "I wish I could do more to help you. I know that I'd be in the way, but I would like to help."

"Just don't let anyone take you." He asked her what she meant. "I don't know. But when the shit hits the fan, they're going to go to desperate measures to get back at us. Hawkins can care for himself, and he's moved back to your parents' house to care for them as well as Dustin. There are men that served under me at other times watching over the others. A nurse has been planted in Boyd's office. Two experts have been put on Parker's farm as hands. Larson has a new secretary that is also a sniper. You're with me."

"I am." She looked at him. "I can shoot, but not well. I do have this amazing cat that can tear into a person, but sadly, he cannot outrun a bullet. He's a mean fucker, but not infallible."

They walked to the deli across from the park. She was just ready to pull off the hat and wig when she saw Wilson walk in with two men that she didn't know. As they took the table next to hers, she reached out and grabbed Colin's hand when he reached for his own hat. Quietly, she told him to listen.

The men were brought their waters and then after they ordered, Wilson started talking in a low tone. Lucky for her, she was able to hear him now, and pulled out a pen to make short notes. Wilson didn't seem to have any idea that she was there, and for that she was grateful.

"I'm telling you right now, if that bitch doesn't die this time, I'm going to go and find her and shoot her myself." The two men with him laughed. "Can you imagine the play we can have on this once she and that other bastard are dead? An American hero is dead, the president did all he could to keep her safe, but the powers that be, they just didn't see it his way. We'd already have it if she didn't seem to have nine fucking lives. Three times over there she got out scot-free, and now we're going to have to take care of her here. I'm telling you right now, that woman is going to pay for this shit she's put us through."

Lauren tried to think what they were talking about. Yes, the last time for sure, but two other times they'd tried to have her killed? She almost missed what one of the other men was saying when she tried to think.

"The houses are all being watched. Phillips, he's got a tail on him too. Gotta find us a runner to keep up with his ass now that he's decided to be some sort of fitness buff. Fucking idiot. All the good health in the world won't keep us from killing him. But he isn't meeting anyone that we can tell. Oh, and that fucking bastard, Wingate, he's whining again, though I have no idea what he has to bitch about. As soon as Irwin is back in that office and I'm vice president, things are gonna change. We're going to start up a war that'll keep us in money for decades with all the kickbacks from that. Cause we all know that war time is the best time." Wilson laughed loudly. "I'm going to take great pleasure in killing Wingate when the time comes."

She looked at Colin when he told her that he'd ordered. The thought of food was going to make her sick right now. These people were insane.

We have to look like we're not doing anything but having lunch. Colin nodded to the table and she saw his phone. *I'm pretty sure that it'll pick up what they're saying. If not, you have your notes. Just pretend that you're having a nice time.*

They mean to kill the VP and then put the country into war. That won't be good for anyone but...but them. Oh Colin, this is worse than we thought. He nodded. *Do you know what that'll do to the...well, everything? It is good to know that he's not in on it. But why kill him? Christ, this is just getting worse and worse all the fucking time.*

I have faith that you'll take care that it doesn't happen. She was glad someone did. *Just do what you can now and we'll work it out later.*

The rest of their conversation was about how they were going to need to get more funding the legal way. One of the men left shortly after their food was brought and they ate it. He'd not said much...very little, as a matter of fact. The other man—his first name was Butch—was apparently expecting some major kickbacks for his part in all this, and Wilson confirmed it. After about another hour of drinking several beers for their lunch, the two of them parted. Hawkins joined Lauren and Colin in the parking lot a few minutes after their sandwiches were wrapped to go and they left the deli.

Chapter 8

Hawkins listened to the recording again. It was hard to hear all of what was being said, but he got most of it. Dustin said he could clean it up a bit, but Hawkins wanted to hear it right now and hadn't let him take it.

"Do you think they know that you were there and wanted you to think this was going on?" He only stared at his dad. "Well, I'm sorry if I want to think that this doesn't go on in real life. These people are talking like it's okay to kill and get away with it. I'm not okay with it, just so you know."

"It does go on all the time, Dad, I'm sorry to say." Hawkins had told his mom and dad what he was doing there when they'd caught him hiding guns all over the place. He'd been surprised when they'd both asked to have a lesson or two on how to use them, and every afternoon since he'd been there he'd taken them out for some target practice. His mom was getting pretty good at it, but his dad could have been a marksman. "Dad, do you think it would be possible to get someone to roam the property a few times a day? I mean, I have a feeling, like Lauren said, they're going to get desperate soon, and we can't have them taking any of you. I worry about you guys going to those houses without me there to watch you."

"I'd rather you were here with your mom. And she said she is not going to help." His dad laughed. "I'm worried that she'll know a great deal more about flipping than Dustin and I do. She's pretty smart, your mother."

"I am at that. What did I do now that has you singing my phrases?" Hawkins told her what they'd been talking about. "Oh yes, I would have some ideas, especially in the outside area. I think you're not putting in enough space in some of backyards. I'd really like to see some trees closer to the house as well. Then there are the bathrooms. Do you have any idea how nice it would be to have a lovely linen closet in every bath? No more of you walking in the hall buck naked looking for a towel that you never seem to remember to before you shower."

Hawkins left them to their argument and went into the office. He wanted to listen to the recording one more time. Before he could get to it, however, Lauren came into the office and he stood up. It was never going to be out of his head that she was his superior no matter how many times she told him to stop it.

"What did you find out from Tony? And how well did he take what you had to say to him?" He sat down when she did and she growled at him. "This is never going to work if you keep doing that. We're family now. You don't have to stand when I'm in the room. Now, what did you find out?"

"He isn't involved, as you had already guessed. I felt sort of bad for him when I told him why you thought the president was involved. I think he's taking that on himself."

She asked him why. "I guess he thought that since he brought you to his attention, then he's the one to blame."

"He's so full of shit. And had he not done that, the president's family would be dead now and the voters wouldn't have known what a shit fuck he is." True, but he doubted that Tony saw it that way. "They're going to try and kill me again. You too, for the sympathy vote. I think Irwin figures that the country will come to their knees when they find out we're dead after making it back here in one…well, sort of one piece."

Hawkins had a feeling that Lauren didn't have as much confidence in herself as she projected on the ground when they were at work. They all had looked up to her for answers, and she'd had them. They rarely didn't work out the way she said, and when they didn't, she asked for their input on how to make it better. She was one hell of a commanding officer, and he'd serve under her for the rest of his life if it was possible. He glanced over at his brother's phone and wondered about a couple of things.

"There's something I wanted to talk to you about. This thing, this conversation between this Butch person and Wilson. What does he mean by trying to kill you off before? I can understand the time in the hospital, but he said three times overseas. One is where they nearly succeeded, but I don't know the other two. Do you know?" She got up to pace and it was all he could do to remain seated. When she stood, he did too; when she sat, so did he. But she was too busy to notice how nervous he was about his inability to be a soldier to her commanding officer. "I've been listening to this thing over and over, and he does say three times. So two if you count the last time."

"Six months before the blow up, remember when we were in that little hotel in Africa? It was down time, they told us. We were so surprised that the order came through that we nearly killed one another to get there. We'd been there about two hours when the water to the hotel was cut off. I don't know if we ever found out what happened, but they moved us to that little house just outside the city."

He remembered. "The hotel blew up. Something about a gas leak." She nodded. "You think that was one of them? They were going to kill us that way?"

"I honestly don't know, but that's one of the times I can think of. I remember now, the hotel guy, he said that he'd been working in the sublevels on something and he was sure he'd cut the line. I believed him and still do. It was just our good fortune that it happened like it did and we were moved. Not so much for his family, but we were out and seemingly safe. For a time anyway."

Hawkins made a note. That left the one. He tried to go back over the last year or so. Things were always happening at some point. A sniper would try to take them out, a truck would run into a building where they were. It was war, shit happened. Then he sat up in his chair.

"The diner. Holy shit, it was the diner." She asked him what he meant. "We'd been in that little town...shit, I don't know the name of it, but this kid came around, remember? He gave us an invite to his parents' diner. Said something like he was a good American, or something like that. Anyway, we were invited to come and eat for free. You said no, but a few of the others went anyway. They were hankering for a meal that didn't come out of a bag and decided to go along anyway."

"Conrad and his cronies." Hawkins nodded and tried to remember the line of events that day. But Lauren remembered for him. "I told him not to go, that no one gave Americans free anything. But he said he'd go and check it out. I said it was an order, that none of us were to go anywhere near that place. I had to go into town too, something from Tony about the next mission. You went with me or…or we might not have been far enough away from it when it went up. Another gas leak, if I remember. That was about the time we picked up those two idiots that got themselves killed too. We would have been there, all of us, when the shit came down."

"Yeah, but I told you that it wasn't gas I was smelling but gasoline. You told me then to keep my mouth shut, that it was none of our business because we'd not been there, none of us had. That was until we found out about Conrad and those other four men. They were killed because he didn't follow orders." He watched her now. Lauren was thinking, something she was good at. "That's it, isn't it? They thought we'd fall for a free meal and we'd be dead. Then again with the hotel. The last time they brought in others to take care of us for them. We both know that the men who trapped us in that building were regular army, like we were. We saw them. They're dead too because someone, the president, wants us dead."

She leaned against the wall and looked at him. Lauren didn't like this any more than he did, but they both knew that they were about the only two in a position to make sure that the men responsible were brought up on charges.

"Tony said they were a part of another cell like us. A group of men who were killed without knowing they were firing on friendlies, or maybe they did. I guess we'll never know that part now." Hawkins had figured that out when Tony had told him that the other men had been ordered to be there like they had been. "Over four dozen men killed, and for what? So some jackass could be voted back in by his unsuspecting public? Then they plunge us into war that will kill even more men and women unnecessarily? Is this what we've come to?"

"I don't know. I wish I did." He knew about the plot to have the president's family killed and that he and Lauren had fucked that up. And he'd been sure there was more to it than simply getting more votes. Now he knew. War. And he was positive that these men were going to go down too, if he had anything to say about it. "And to be honest, Lauren, I'm not sure that even knowing the answers will make this any easier to swallow."

"Hawkins, why are we even doing this? I mean, not trying to save our asses, but the world in general? It's as if for one step we take forward, there are three more that go back on us. I'm sorta getting sick of this shit." He could understand her frustration probably more than most could have. "I want to quit. All of it, right now."

"Me too. But we can't let them win." When she didn't say anything, he thought about what he'd been doing before joining the service. "When I was seventeen, I met this woman. She was brave, smart, and somewhat of a dick, actually. Then she told me what she did every day of her life, every time she rolled out of her bunk, how her day went. I could see the gleam in her eyes from how excited she'd been to do whatever had been asked of her, and I wanted that."

"I should have talked you out of it." He laughed and so did she. "If I had just let you talk to the others, some ass that had a quota to hit and not me, you might not have been hurt or in the middle of a big fucking shit storm."

"Yeah, maybe. But then I wouldn't have met you. Got to know you in ways that my brother never will. Seen you in action, working through a problem like no one else would. And you will solve this one too. I have faith in you."

She told him she wasn't so sure. "Yes, you will. All you have to do is think what they're going to do next. And being as stupid as they are, that won't be too hard."

The phone rang on the desk and neither of them answered it. He supposed he could. It was his parents' house, but he didn't live there full-time, and as far as he knew, no one knew he was there. So when it was cut off, no doubt from someone else answering it, he pulled out the files that they'd accumulated over the last few days. Colin came in just as he was ready to start pinning them to the wall board that had been brought in.

"Pete is missing." Hawkins stood up and reached for his sidearm. He'd taken to wearing it in the open the last few days so that everyone could see that he was comfortable with it. "He left the house this morning to run some errands for his mom and hasn't called or returned. When they reach for him, they get nothing. They're calling for you to help."

Hawkins watched Lauren go from insecure mode to hit-the-floor-running Burcher in a heartbeat. As she started barking orders, he smiled. This was the Major he knew and respected. But then he supposed everyone had an off day, and this had been hers. Hawkins heard his name and paid attention. To not do so would get him killed.

"Hawkins, call Tony on the cell and tell him everything we know. Colin, call Bear. Let him know that I need him there. And Sheppard. They're both good at tracking and can see what we can't." Colin nodded when Lauren started barking orders at him. "I'll go to the house now and see what they have on where he might have been going, and some of his friends."

Hawkins knew that Bear was literally a bear shifter and had retired from the navy a few years earlier. Sheppard had never been in the service, but he'd done some work for them when they needed it. He would follow them, in his own transportation most of the time, and help Lauren get info that she needed. He wasn't exactly orthodox when it came to getting the information either. He was...he did things his own way.

Hawkins was just hanging up the phone when Lauren left him and Colin to run to her parents' house. He knew as surely as she did that had her parents just let them put a man on them, Pete would be safe, but there was no time for them to go back and redo it. Not that they ever could. Lauren was making a list of help that would scare the average man. He almost felt sorry for the shits that had taken the younger man. Hawkins looked at his brother when he said his name.

"She'll get him back, won't she?" Hawkins said that they all would. "I'm...I feel useless with this kind of thing. I want to help her, but I don't have a clue how. She's never made me feel that way, but I guess my head is making me this way."

"You are helping her, Colin. Just by not questioning her every move and trying to be all protective of her. If anyone does not need you to be all overly protective, it's her. She's got this, even though it might not look like she does. I swear to you, she knows what the hell she's doing." Colin nodded. "I won't let her get hurt. I'll watch her for you. Hell, she'll be watching all of us more than she will herself."

"I know that about her too. And I don't want either of you to get hurt. None of us, as a matter of fact." Hawkins said he understood that. "Tony, this guy, you trust him not to be one of the bad guys? She does, but what do you think?"

"I think that if she trusts someone, you should take it as gospel that they're trustworthy. And if she tells you to kill someone, even someone that you think is your best friend, then blow their fucking head off. She knows that too." Colin said he wasn't sure he could do that. "If it comes to a choice as to who you want to save, it's not a problem. Trust me, I know that."

"You did a great deal of killing, didn't you, Hawkins?" He didn't answer him. Sometimes the best answer was no answer at all. "I'm glad, more than you can know, that you're safe and that Lauren has your back."

"You have no idea how true those words are, Colin. Lauren is the best that there is, hands down." Colin said nothing, but stared at the phone in his hand for several seconds. "We'll get him back. He might be a little beat to shit when we do, but he'll come back to them."

"I know." Then Colin looked at him with a strange smile. "I can almost feel sorry for those who dared fuck with her family. Almost. They're going to pay big time for touching one of hers, aren't they?"

"You got that right."

Hawkins was going to meet Bear at the gate of the land. Then the two of them were going to run over to the Burcher's. They were going to make sure no one tried to get to them while Lauren got her brother back. Colin was right, they were going to pay for this.

~~~

Pete tried to see where he was, but all he could make out was a blur and some light. Not a lot of it, but enough to give him an idea that he was in a room with a window rather than the car trunk that he'd been in. Plus, he was no longer being tossed around like a sock in a dryer either. That certainly helped his sore head.

What are you trying to do, drive me nuts? What the hell were you thinking, getting caught like this? He smiled at the sound of Lauren's voice in his head. *Have I not told you over and over, never get in the cars of strangers, and most certainly don't get your ass kidnapped? You think I have time for this shit? I don't, just so you know.*

I love you too, big sister. But so you know, I'm not all macho like you are. I'm just a poor lowly cat that has a pounding headache. He was relieved that she was home to come and get him. *Tell Mom I love her. And Dad too.*

Bullshit. You tell them yourself, moron. You sound like you're ready to give up. You'd better fucking not, if you don't want me to kick your ass. We're not to the point where you're going to die, you hear me? And won't be so long as I'm alive. Which I might add isn't going to be long for the jackoffs that took you. He believed her too. *Do you have any idea where you might be? When they stuffed your ass in that car, we kinda lost track of you. So we're relying on shit here to find you.*

No. But I have been thinking about all the crap you told me. And so you know, I know it's not crap now. She'd been drilling in his head since he'd been a kid to be aware of his surroundings, that even a smell could be the difference between him eating or not. *I can smell mold. Not much to go on, but that's what I smell. And I can hear traffic.*

Honey, mold is everywhere. Can you tell me what kind of mold it is? And a lot of traffic, or just an occasional car? He told her a lot, and big rigs too. He also told her that he had no idea about the mold either. *Good, sounds like a highway. Okay, mold. Are you on a mattress or floor?*

Floor. Yeah, I thought of that too. Maybe I was smelling my bedding, but there is none. And I can't see either. I was hit pretty hard in the head and now things are slightly blurry. There's a little light, but I can't tell for sure if it's a window or a lightbulb. She asked him how many men had taken him. *I don't know.*

Two for sure. One of them stopped me as I was coming out of the market and asked me for directions. When I turned to show him by pointing where he needed to be, I felt my head explode. That's when I saw the second guy. There might have been a third, but I don't know for sure. And before you ask me, no, I didn't know any of them. Not by scent or face.

There are three, we think, but weren't sure if there were others that didn't touch anything. When they took you, they left the bat behind. It has three scents on it that Bear is looking for now. He didn't know who Bear was, but whatever it took to get him back. *Pete, you have a tracker on you, but I can't find it working. They either took it out or something happened to it when they tossed you in the car. Are you on your back or on your belly? I need you to be on your back. Maybe it's a matter of your body blocking it out.*

I'm on my belly. Let me turn over in a second. My hands and feet are tied, but I think I can do it. Can this tracking thing find me through concrete? She told him she wasn't sure what it would do, as she'd not had much to do with it other than putting it on his chain a few days ago. He tried his best to roll over without crying out in pain while she told him it was a cheap one since Mom and Dad didn't want him to even have that. *I bet they want me to have it now. Oh, and the floor is made of concrete. And though I can't see well, I can make out cinder block. I think I'm in a cinderblock room.*

Okay, good to know. He could see something else and wondered if he was seeing things. He told her what he thought he could see. *Carnival things? You mean like rides and shit or floats? I don't know, is there a storage place around here for parade shit when it's done?*

Ask Dad, he might know. He tried to see past the doorway where he as, but it was making him sick to his stomach. *Lauren, are you going to get me out of here? If you are, then I will owe you for the rest of my life. I don't want to die in this place. I can almost see the headlines now...Pete Burcher dies with a clown hanging over his head.*

You're not going to die, and I love clowns. I want you to lie very still and listen for me. Do you hear voices? Close your eyes and concentrate on anything you can hear. Sounds of people talking and nothing else. He wanted to tell her that his head hurt too much to concentrate on anything, but he did as she asked.

Her calming voice telling him to block out certain sounds like cars and trucks helped a great deal. The sound of birds, if there were any, was the next thing he was to block out. Then she told him to breathe slowly, not to listen with his heart but his senses. Finally, he thought he heard someone.

I hear voices. Two of them I think. They're talking about you. She said that she was really popular like that. *No, I don't think they're enamored of you. More like they hate you and want you out of the picture kind of feelings. I don't know the voice, but I can hear them pretty well.*

I don't care about their love or hate of me for the moment. I'm more concerned about getting you home. Okay, Pete, I want you to listen to how many voices you hear. You hear two...are you sure that there aren't three? And Dad says that there are two places where they store left over floats, and they're both near a highway. You have to work with me to narrow down which one you're at. He closed his eyes again and thought about the voices. *You're doing a great job. We've gotten so much closer to you than we were.*

Voices. Okay. There are two...wait, no three. But the third one, I don't think he knows the other two. She asked him why he thought that. But before he could answer her, he heard the sound of a gunshot. *I think they killed him, Lauren. He was asking them what they were doing here and I think they killed him. Christ, Lauren, they're going to kill me.*

No, they're not. I'm coming, Pete. All right? I got it now. I know where you are. Sit tight. He asked her how she knew. *I heard the shot, so I know just where you are. I'm coming for you now.*

Pete could have cried. He didn't. Grown men didn't cry, but he was so relieved that he had to lay there and fight with the feeling he wasn't going to be dead in a few minutes. She was close, his mind kept telling him. Lauren was close, and she was going to come for him. Even when he heard the door near him open, he knew that she was going to save his ass.

The shots being fired did terrify him a little. Every time he flinched away from the sound, he knew more places where he hurt. Moving again, he tried to get as far from the light as he could without crying out in pain. His hands being tied made things hard, but he finally felt the wall behind him and he didn't move. Then something in front of him stood in his line of sight, and he tried his best not to yell for his sister. He wasn't sure if someone had walked in front of the light or if there was someone in the room with him, but he didn't as much as whimper.

"Mother fuck, how the hell did she find us?" He'd heard the voice earlier but didn't answer when he started saying his name quietly. "Pete? Damn it, boy, you can't still be out. We didn't hit you that—"

The gunshot so close startled him, but he didn't move. He wasn't sure who was doing the shooting, but he was hoping it was Lauren. Then someone touched his head. There was no way he could have stopped the cry of pain when they touched his wound that he'd had no idea was there until then.

"I got you." Lauren. It was his Lauren. "Come on now. I don't know if there is anyone else here, and I have to get you out to Colin. He's sort of pissy I made him stay behind."

He felt the tape at his hands being cut away. Then his legs were free. Lauren told him to move slowly so as not to hurt himself. Then she helped him to stand, holding onto him until the pins and needles that felt like they were all over his body moved away. He'd never been so glad to have a big sister as he was at that very moment.

"You're very bossy. Does he know this? I mean, I can have a talk with him if you want. Sort of give him a heads up to some of your more violent moods. You have them, you know." She told him she thought he was getting it, but thanked him all the same. "I should have a talk with him anyway. When you get us out of here."

"We're going. And don't tell him everything. We need some mystery, I think." She let him lean heavily on her after he nearly fell atop her when he took his first step. His head was making him sick now, and he told her he didn't know if he could see well enough to help her. And she told him that shifting right now was not an option. They didn't know who might be with them. "I'm not taking you to the hospital. I think I'd like for whoever took you to think you're still kidnapped. At least for a while."

"Man-napped." She asked him what he meant. "I'm not a kid. So it has to be man-napped."

"All right, I don't want anyone who helped man-nap you to know you're free right away. I'm thinking they might already know, but that's fine too. You're safe and the bad guys aren't." He started to ask her about that, but decided he really didn't want to know.

He was glad that his vison was off when they walked out of his cell. As they made their way by two bodies, he was pretty sure that one of them had their head taken off and the other had a neat hole in his forehead. The third man, the one in his cell, had been shot too, but he'd been too busy trying to get up on his feet to look. He was pretty sure that she'd shot him in the head too, however. It seemed to be her mode of doing things.

"It is." He asked her what she meant. "My mode of killing people. In the head, and they don't get up and try to kill you again. Once in the head and no more brain function. Not that these guys had much of that going for them anyway. But there you have it."

"I didn't know I said that out loud."

By the time he finished his statement, they were going through a door and into the bright sunlight. Lifting his arm up caused him a great deal of pain, but he felt himself being lifted and knew that Colin had him. As he was set gently in the back of the car, Pete started to sob. He was safe. He hated that he was crying like a big baby, but he'd been as close to being killed as he'd ever been in his life, and it sort of played badly in his head.

No one said anything as they got in the front seat. He was given a box of tissues and a phone and told to call home, but it took him several times before he thought he could without breaking down again. But it was for nothing. As soon as he heard his mom's voice, Pete started crying like a baby again. All he could think about was that he wasn't dead and that Lauren had saved him.

Chapter 9

"The first man you sent the prints for is a hit man that we've been trying to get for five years. His name, or one of them that he goes by, is Vicious. His real name must have sounded too tame for him, so he changed it to that from Bob Winder." Tony looked at the pictures of the dead man that had accompanied the fingerprints. He'd had his head taken off. And he didn't want to think of the rage that had made her do that to him. He supposed he might have done the same had it been his family, but Christ, she was good at what she did. Scary good. "The second man is one of the lesser of the two. And by lesser I mean that his rap sheet isn't nearly as long. You name it, these two have done it. Ruben Waitsfield started out his career as a killer at the prime age of ten, killing his stepfather and mother in what they thought was self-defense."

"Let me guess, they treated him badly and he had to fight back." Tony smiled at Lauren's tone. She of all people would know about abusive parents. "So this other guy, do you have anything on him?"

"Yes." He didn't want to tell her. It was going to royally piss her off. "He's army. One of your previous men. But I think you might have known that, didn't you?"

"Yeah, I thought so. Mitch Decker." He nodded, then realized they were on the phone and told her it was him. "Dishonorably discharged about four or five years ago. He said that he'd get me in time. It's amazing what people think you owe them when they don't succeed in cutting your throat while you lay slumbering in your bunk. He'd been a little pissy with me because I had the nerve to stop his little dope ring he had going on the side while working with me. Fucking moron. Where do we get these people, anyway? They should let me screen them. I could narrow out the idiots. I certainly couldn't do any worse."

"I doubt they'd let you do it your way even if that was an option." She snorted and Tony laughed. "I wanted to thank you again for helping me get here. I'm not sure what else they'll find, but that bug in my bathroom freaked me out a bit. Who wants to watch me take a shit?"

Tony looked around the hotel room that he'd been in since yesterday. His house was being de-bugged, but not the kind of de-bugging that required the men that one called in for insects. His was literally being de-bugged of all traces of the monitors and other shit that had been hidden away in his house for who knew how long. Victoria had found a stash of them, and she'd been hard pressed not to go after those who had dared invade his home. And she'd told him she was his mate.

He'd known that, of course. Not that day, but a couple of hours later when all the stuff that had gone on that day in the bathroom stall had settled. They'd spent an enjoyable evening together after making love several times and played chess. He supposed *settled* was the wrong term, but he'd come to terms with what was going on. And now, he had himself a mate to lean on as well.

"This is just one more nail in the coffin for them. You know that, right? And the fact that they thought they could come after Pete is going to cost them as well. By the way, Dad heard from them this morning. Seems they found traces of his blood in a warehouse where three dead men were. He said he had no idea what they were talking about, that his son was right there. He's pretty pissed, more than I've ever seen him."

Tony wasn't going to ask. Lauren told him that the further he stayed away from what she did to get this done the safer he'd be. And Victoria was helping them. Everyone wanted this to end, and end where no more men were killed unless they brought it on to themselves.

"What do you need for me to do?" He heard her heavy sigh and knew that whatever it was, she didn't want to ask for it. "Lauren, I need to help you. I'm feeling a little left out of this, and if you want to know the truth, I want their asses as badly as you do. They killed a lot of good men for no good reason."

"I know you do. But there is one thing I have to do that you can't be involved in. There might still be a chance that I'm wrong about those who are involved." He doubted that and said that to her. "Yeah, I don't think so either, but I'm putting mine and Hawkins's ass on the line with this. Once they have me where they think they want me, Hawkins and I are going to commit treason. Once that hits the fan, you're going to be asked a shit load of questions I don't want you to know the answer for."

"You're going to take the VP." She didn't say anything. "All right. I understand. Just let me know when you need me to stand down."

"Today."

Then the line went dead. She was going to do it now. And he'd bet his entire retirement that it was nearly in the works now, if not already executed. He just hoped the girl was right. If not, she was going to stand before a firing squad, and he'd hate to be the man who told her mate it was going to happen.

He was still working on the paperwork that she'd given him to sort out when he heard someone outside of his door. He wasn't too terribly worried, but still pulled his firearm out and had it at his side. If they were coming in without permission, he was going to kill them and ask questions later. The small sound and the pain was all the warning he got before he found himself on the floor and bleeding. He looked at the large hole in the door where he'd been standing and realized he'd been shot. Fuckballs, he'd been shot was all he could think of.

Getting up as best he could, he reached for Victoria. She said his name in that sultry voice of hers, and he was shocked when his cock stretched in his pants. Then she said his name again, this time with more urgency.

I'm shot. She said she was coming for him. *I don't know who it is or why they did it. Perhaps we should wait and see.*

Victoria was there, her hand over his wound, when the door slammed against the inner wall. Before he could lift his weapon, even if he could, the men, two of them, were gone. Just simply gone. Then Victoria was back at his side. Tony looked up at her and could see blood on her mouth. When she licked it away and winked at him, he knew that she'd just saved his life by killing the bastard that had shot him.

"What do you need of these things?" He told her all of it. "I'll have someone take it back with us then. Rosen will gather it for you and keep it safe."

"I'm dying." She told him he wasn't, but he knew better. His chest was bleeding a lot more than he'd thought it should. "I wanted to tell you that I love you."

"And I you. But you will not die." She looked down at his chest then back to his face. "How do you feel about being a night walker as I am? We could have such fun together."

"I don't want to die." She lifted him up and he moaned. "Victoria, I'm too heavy for you. And I don't want to die, but you can't be carrying me around like a pillow."

"Hush now. I'm doing the right thing. I don't normally do that, but you'll let me by being quiet. Rosen is here. He is gathering this up for you now." He could hear the sirens in the distance. "You will be talked about, I'm afraid. But there is little we can do about it now. I'm taking you to my home where I can help you."

He wasn't sure what she was talking about. As his life began to fade, the memories of his childhood and those memories with his wife began to surge forward. Sex in the bathroom with Victoria. Their long talks and his love for her. The Christmas when he got his first gun, the day he'd met Lauren. Memories never repeated themselves. He was an older man but the memories burned behind his eyes like a projector in a movie theater. And Tony was afraid. More than he'd ever been in his lifetime.

The softness of a mattress touched his back, and even though it was perhaps the softest thing he'd ever felt, he still moaned. Pain, the inability to breathe well, made him hurt in places he thought were not connected to him that way. Seeing Victoria above him, Tony reached up to touch her face, but all he was able to do was flop his arm at her.

"I've fallen in love with you, my dear. Too late now, but I wanted you to know." She told him it wasn't too late for them. "I'm afraid it is."

The taste of blood filled his mouth. He felt a pinch at his wrist as he swallowed her elixir. Dreams began to fade, as did the memories. Tony felt his heart skip several beats and tears flood his eyes at all he was going to miss. For the first time in his life, he'd found love, a love that should have lasted for decades, and some prick had shot him.

"Drink," she told him in her soft sexy voice. "I've plans for you later, and you cannot perform well if you are too weak to play."

He was pretty sure he was already past the point of playing. His eyes began to close as he felt his heart take a new twist. Not painfully so, but enough to make him think he was given something stronger to bring him around. Then Tony opened his eyes once more and looked at his Victoria.

"I love you." She told him that she loved him as well. "I wish I could have met you sooner. Years ago."

"We have plenty of time now, my love. As much as we will ever want." His befuddled mind thought he'd misheard her, and she'd said, "We had plenty of time." As his eyes closed for the final time, Tony wondered how Lauren would finish her job. And how she'd take him being dead. His heart hurt for the younger woman.

"Yes, I understand." Lauren leaned her head against the wall. Tony was presumed dead. His body was missing, but the amount of blood in the room led them to believe that he'd crawled away and died elsewhere. The police and the army were out looking for him.

"I'm very sorry for your loss." Lauren didn't answer the president. Even now, she knew his words were fake, not a hint of sincerity. "He was a good man, and I think we'll feel his loss for years to come."

"He was the best man I ever knew. To be shot like that in a hotel room on American soil is not the way I ever thought he'd go." The man at the other end of the phone said that he was a great American. "Yes. He was. How much effort are you putting into finding out who shot him? I'd like to be on that taskforce."

Lauren knew just where Tony was, and how he'd gotten there. Early that morning, well before most people were up and about, Victoria had come to her and told her what she knew. Rosen had brought with him all the things that had been in Tony's hotel room when he'd been shot.

"He reached for me...even in his last moments he reached out to me to tell me he'd been hurt. I could not leave him there if I could have a chance to save him." Lauren told her that she understood. That she had loved him as well. "He's not dead, darling. He's no longer just a cat either, because I gave him my blood. I gave him a great deal. If he is converted, then he'll be what I am with a little extra, but he won't die. And he's safe. As safe as you are now."

The relief had been profound. She'd sobbed for over ten minutes, not realizing how much she really did love the man. He was a pain in her ass, but he was a good friend. And would continue to be so, thanks to Victoria.

"The police are looking into it. Do you suppose they'll catch the man soon?" Lauren forgot about the president and turned to look at Colin when he laughed softly. "It would be a nice thing to tell his widow when we do."

It was too much for her. This man had tried to have his family killed, then her because she'd had the nerve to intercede on their part. And all those men, most of them her friends, were dead because of him. Before she could think to curb her temper or her mouth, she blasted him.

"His wife has been gone for ten years, so I doubt much that she'll care. And his son died when he was three, in the event you think he might care either." It was cold, yes, but she hated this man more than she did anything in the world. And Lauren blamed him for Tony being hurt. "But I care that we find the person responsible for this. And I plan on looking into this too. No matter what it takes or who I have to take down to get justice for him."

"Well now, Lauren dear, we don't want to step on anyone's toes over this. Let the police handle this. You just sit back and rest. We need you healthy. As for my not knowing about his wife, I'm sorry about that. I guess my files aren't as up to date as yours might be." The low growl came from the pit of her belly and spilled from her mouth just as Colin put his hand around her waist and held her. "Are you unwell?"

"I'm fine." The bitter bite of her words burned her. She let out a long, slow breath when Colin bit gently on her shoulder. "I have to go."

Tossing the phone in the general direction of the desk, she turned to face Colin. She needed him, right now, and tore at his clothing when he seemed content to just touch her. When his shirt was hanging limply from the top of his pants, she leaned to his chest and bit down on his hard nipple. His growl had her looking up at him.

"Strip." *Gladly*, she thought, and started to pull off her blouse. But like her, his need was somewhat out of control and he tore her blouse and bra off her even as he lifted her up high enough that her breasts were even with his mouth. As soon as he suckled at her, she cried out with the tight hard punch of the climax it gave her.

The wall touched her bare back, and she loved the roughness of it as he devoured her. When he lifted her higher, his tongue in her navel, she held him to her, begging him to take her now. It was as if a trigger had been switched on and the need to be fucked was the only way to turn it off.

When he set her on her feet, she whimpered when he took a step back from her and told her to take the rest of her clothing off. Taking off what was left of her shirt and then her pants, she stood before him in her panties. He watched her as she spread her hands over her belly then moved them slowly down to her pussy.

"I'm wet. Can you smell me?" He said that he could and loved the smell. "Take off your pants, Colin. I want to taste you like you have me."

"If you suck me off, I'm going to take you against that desk harder than you've ever been fucked before. I need to dominate you. My cat, he wants his taste too." Her pussy flooded at his words and she slid her hand into her panties, then into her pussy. Letting her feelings come out in her moans, she moaned several more times as he unbuckled his belt, then pulled it free of the loops. "Come for me, Lauren. Then lick your cream from your fingers for me."

She touched her clit as he pulled his pants free of his body. His boxers were wet at the tip of his cock, which was straining hard against the silk material. As soon as he rubbed his hand over his cock and moaned, Lauren came again, this time saying his name over and over as her fingers were drenched with her cream.

Slowly she moved up her body, which was still trembling with the power of her release, and rubbed her cream over her nipples before touching her tongue with her wet fingers. Colin watched her, his hand going faster and faster up and down his shaft as he did. When she stuck her fingers into her mouth and sucked them, he let his cat take him and knocked her back against the wall again.

The cat was merciless. He tore at her panties and spit them out even as she spread her legs for him. He nipped several times at her clit, bringing her twice more as he lapped at her. And when her knees could no longer hold her up, she slid down the wall and let him eat her as much as he wanted. The moment that Colin took back his body, she felt her pussy ripen for him, swell with a need she'd never experienced before.

"I want to fuck you." Looking down at Colin as he ate her as his cat had, she nodded. "Next time you can suck me, baby. But I need to fuck you. Now. Turn over for me."

She moved to roll to her knees, her hands braced on either side of her. When she felt Colin at her backside, she cried out with anticipation. When his hand came down on her ass, gently, like a soft feather over her, Lauren begged him to take her.

"I'm going to fuck you slowly, baby. I want to feel you tighten around me twice before I fill you." Lauren whimpered again, begged him to give her relief now. "You'll enjoy this more, I swear it."

"Colin, I'm going to murder you in your sleep if you don't fuck me now." His cock slamming into her pussy took her breath away. And when he moved, jerking back then slamming forward again, she screamed out her release.

It was powerful but yet not satisfying. He was holding back, not giving her what she needed. As she worked her ass back, trying her best to take him deeper, he chuckled, and she knew right then she was going to get her gun and blow his dick right off. Then he did the most extraordinary thing: he pulled her body up off the floor and sat her on his cock while he fondled her breasts. She was sitting on him, his body holding hers, not just with his hands but his cock too. She was impaled over him and felt it all the way to the back of her throat.

"Come for me this way. I want to see your face when you do." She opened her eyes, not even realizing that she'd closed them, and saw the mirror across from them. As his finger slid into her, joining his cock at her pussy, she watched as his free hand cupped her breast. "Come now, Lauren; let me see your face when you do."

It wasn't a matter of not doing as he requested. It was powerful, her climax, so much so that it tore from her body and seemed to be poised there for just a second before it took her again. There was nothing to stop the onslaught of emotions that filled her. The pleasure was death defying in that it seemed to give her small heart attacks with each beat of her heart. And when he bit into her shoulder, the pain of it had her reaching out for something, anything to hold onto, and she wrapped her hands over his. Lauren was falling even as he told her he was coming too.

When she woke, not only was she in bed but Colin was curled up beside her. The room was brightly lit by the sunlight that seemed to stream in more and more daily. Rolling to her back, she looked into his eyes as he smiled at her.

"You're very impatient. Has anyone ever told you that before?" She told him most days. "I love you, Lauren. I love you with all my heart."

"And I love you." She rolled to her side again and looked around the room that was beginning to look homier every day. "We need more furniture in this place. Last night when your parents came over, we only had enough chairs for three people."

"I'd love to help you out with that, but I have to go back to the plant today. They're having issues that I started to work on but now I need to go and fix." She turned back to look at him. "And I know you have that appointment with the company doctor. Have you decided what you're going to say to him when he tries to tell you that you're no longer fit to work?"

"I guess killing him isn't going to work for you." He shook his head and laughed. "Yeah, Tony said not to as well. But I will try and figure out who he's on the payroll for. I mean, I know, but I want to find out who else is playing me."

"Will you be armed when you go in?" She told him she was forever armed, and to prove her point, she reached up under the pillow they were sharing and showed him her weapon. "I see. And what if I had found that thing and accidently shot you with it?"

"Nope. You know better. I get pissy when I'm hurt." He got up and she noticed that he was nearly dressed. "I guess it's later than I thought it was. What time will you be back?"

"Around five or so. If I'm going to be later, I'll call you." He turned to her as he was tying his tie. "Or you could meet me in town for dinner. We've never had a date. This could be fun."

"All right." She got up and stretched. His growl had her turning to him. "You're the one that put me here naked. Next time perhaps you could throw a shirt over me or something."

"I like you naked. It makes making love to you so much easier." He was pulling on his jacket when he turned to her again. "Pete called too. He wants to talk to you about something that happened. He called while you were sleeping. I asked him if I could help and he said no, it was for you."

"I'm sorry, Colin. I'll have a talk with him about being rude." He told her he wasn't rude, but had told him that he had to talk to her and that was fine. "I told him to think about things when they took him. He might have remembered something that he thinks is important." Pete hadn't left his house since the day he'd been brought there by her. Lauren had spoken to their parents a few times, and they were now working with them instead of against them about keeping them safe. "Dad said that he's doing well. Did he sound okay to you?"

"Yes. Perfectly fine. He said that he's been in the yard a few times, so you know. And that tomorrow he's going to go to town with Hawkins. Hawkins said that Pete is suffering with fear badly, and that getting him out will be the best thing for him." Hawkins would know. He'd had a big fear too after the first time he'd been shot. She'd bullied him much like she'd bet he was going to do to Pete. "I'll call you when I get to the plant. Be careful today, and please don't kill anyone or make me have to come and bail you out of jail, all right?"

"I'm not making promises, but I will try to be good." She'd had him remove the tags in her body a few days ago. Boyd had been there as well, and he'd said that Colin had done a good job, and she didn't even have a single scar to show for it. The only time she'd taken them out of her pocket was when she'd gone to find her brother. Today they were going to be shoved down someone's throat. Or so she hoped.

As she showered, she thought of all the shit she had to do today. First she had to see the company doctor. Then she had some errands to run, such as stopping by the bank to get the paperwork started to put Colin on the accounts she had. And then there was the appointment with her attorney. Something that she knew had to be done, but nothing she was looking forward to. He was forever telling her that she needed to invest in this or that, and she was just fine in the few companies that she was in.

While in the kitchen, she was startled to hear someone pull into the drive. The sticker on the side of the car stated that they were a religious group that apparently thought a glowing cross was perfect for a logo. She supposed it was if dayglow green was a good color.

Standing just to the right of the door, she watched the two men get out and wander around like they were glad to see the bushes by her front door. Then when the younger of the two knocked, she saw his gun. Either religion had changed a great deal since she'd been away or these men were not what they had written on the side of their vehicle.

Pulling out her weapon and holding it in front of her like she knew what she was doing, Lauren opened the door just before they could ring the bell. The bigger of the two men and the older reached into his jacket, and Lauren shot between his open legs. Neither man moved after that.

"What the fuck are you doing here?" When they didn't answer, she shot the younger one in the leg. As he dropped, she pointed her weapon at the other man. "You'll notice I'm not the sociable type. If you don't answer the question, the next one is going to take your head off."

"Can I see to my partner and call for an ambulance?" She told him only if he wanted it to be his final act on this earth. "You weren't supposed to be able to get up and around. Someone is lying on your behalf. That was really shitty of them, don't you think?"

"Yeah, I get that a lot. I suppose it's my charming way of opening my door. What the fuck are you doing here? I'm gonna count to five, then I'm going to start removing parts of your skull with my weapon. One. Two."

The younger man started talking. "We got a contract that said to kill you. And anyone else that was in the house too. This was going to be my first one. They never said you'd be able to shoot back. That's really fucked up."

Lauren shot the kid in the head. Then she looked at the other man. He looked like he was going to lunge at her and she smiled at him. This was a good deal more fun than she'd thought it would be.

"Who took out the hit?" No answer, so she shot him in the shoulder. "See how this works? I ask a question, you answer. If not, then I shoot. I have no qualms whatsoever in killing you too. I had a really long list of shit that I had to do today, and you've put me behind. Who hired you and that idiot there?"

"You are as cold and heartless as they said you were." She thanked him. "I didn't mean it as a compliment. You really are a fucking cunt, aren't you?"

"Oh, really? Well how sad. Because to me, it was a compliment. And yeah I am, probably worse too if you want to know the truth. Now answer the question before I kill you." He asked her if she really could, and for an answer, she shot him again, this time in the leg where it knocked him to the ground. "Who did you get the contract from?"

"Goes by the name Briggy. Not a very scary name. Maybe he should come and talk to you about being scary." She asked him if he was scared. "Yes. I am. You're going to kill me anyway, aren't you?"

"Yes." He nodded and slowly moved his hand into his pocket. If he pulled a gun, this conversation was going to end now, but he took out an envelope and held it out to her. "What is it?"

"In addition to a picture of you and the men that you work with, there is the entire conversation that this Briggy person and I had." She asked him why he had it on him. "Because unlike the man here, I figured we were gonna be shot to shit anyway. Just never figured you'd get the jump on us, and we'd be able to take a little of you with us when we went."

"Yeah, life sucks like that." Lauren reached for Hawkins and asked him to come to her. Then she told Colin what she was up to. He asked her if she was all right. *I am. They're both...well, one is dead, and the other might make it if he doesn't piss me off. Are you coming home?*

Yes. I've already turned around. She told him to wait until the police passed him. *Why? I mean, I'd feel a good deal better if I was there with you now and not waiting around. If you know what I mean?*

I do, but I think it will play better if the fuckwads that run this town think I was the poor helpless woman at home alone. He laughed and told her she was far from helpless. *Yeah, I know that, but they seem to think I need protecting. Besides, I'm not sure who I can trust in the department as yet.*

Colin told her that the police just passed him and he'd wait five minutes. Holding her weapon on the man as he lay on her porch, she asked him if he was going to tell the police what he'd been doing there.

"Will you kill me if I say no?" She said that she might anyway, but no, not if he was going to tell the truth. "Got nothing to live for. Once this gets out, that man that hired me, if he wants someone like you dead, then I'm not long for this world anyway. To be honest, I'd rather go out by your hand. I think it would be quicker."

She never got the chance to tell him she wasn't going to do it. The police and Hawkins came into the yard just as she held her weapon up and her finger off the guard and went to her knees. Lauren was tossed to the ground just as three police started to scream at her and the other man to drop their weapons.

Some days, she thought, it wasn't worth getting out of the fucking bed.

KATHI S. BARTON

Chapter 10

Jarvis Wingate moved from his living room to his kitchen and was just pulling down a cup to have a nice hot brew when something poked him in the back of the head. He'd been in the service and had been around guns his entire life before that. He stilled when the gun poked harder at his head.

"I don't have any money here." He did, but he figured if the guy was going to rob him, he'd have him lead him right to his own stash of weapons. He felt the man's breath on his cheek before he spoke.

"It's Hawkins. Don't move." He didn't so much as nod at the man. "You're being watched, did you know that?"

"Figures." He felt the weapon leave his head, and he started to turn when he was told to finish what he was doing. "You mean my tea?"

As they were both whispering, Jarvis thought that Hawkins hadn't heard him and asked again. The man laughed and told him to pretend he wasn't there.

"Yeah, we both know that's not going to happen. Have you been sent here to kill me? There is a lot of that going around." Hawkins said he wasn't. "Then I can only assume that you're here for something else. Like...I have no idea. Too scared to think beyond you're not here to kill me. Can I fix you a cup of tea, young man? I feel as if I need to do something, or just crawl in the corner with my thumb in my mouth."

"I told you I wasn't going to hurt you and I won't. You're not my target in all this. But this is the only room that only has one camera. It's pointed, for some reason, at your fridge." Jarvis waited for the water to boil in the water pot and thought about what he'd just said. "Yes, before you ask, they're in the bathrooms as well. Mostly pointed at the sink."

"Good to know the next time I have to take a crap." He was trying for humor and knew that it fell short of the mark. "Why are you here if not to kill me? I have to tell you, if they were to send in your boss, Lauren, I'd have shit myself by now. She's dangerous."

"She sent me while she takes care of other things. I'm going to kidnap you. With your permission." The tea bag that he was dunking in the now hot water stilled. "Keep doing it, sir, and I'll explain the best I can. But you're going to have to trust me a little here."

"Lauren sent you." He said that she had. "And let me guess, Joe has something to do with you being here in the middle of the night and thinking to kidnap me. I'm assuming that this is to keep someone else from coming in here and killing me."

"Yes, it is. They want you dead." He asked him who the *they* was. "Brigadier General Wilson and the president."

Jarvis sat at his little table, careful to keep his face out of the direction of the refrigerator. He'd had a feeling that he was being left out of something, and now he knew why.

Not really why, he supposed, but at least someone was watching out for him. He quietly asked Hawkins if he could explain things for him.

"They figure you're in the way of their plans. I'm not entirely sure what their plans are, but they mean to kill you, thus making Wilson the VP in the next round of elections. The plan, as we know it so far, is to kill Lauren and me and use that as a way for voters to see him as a compassionate man. Some bullshit about how we were serving our country, and now we had only come home to die. By the way, they think that I've lost an arm due to the injuries over there. I've been keeping a low profile." Jarvis said he'd heard that today, that he'd lost his arm. "Today someone by the hang tag of Briggy sent two men to see Lauren and to kill her and Colin. Didn't work. She killed one and injured the other. He had a lot of paperwork on him but no name that the police can use. But she can and will find them. You need to be put up before that happens."

"Briggy, as I'm sure you've guessed, is Wilson. He told me that once. For some reason he thought it was fucking funny that no one would ever guess it was him. He's a moron, in the event you didn't already know that." Hawkins said they had thought so. "So, how does this work now? You beat me up a little, then take me out of here so they can see it?"

"No. I'm going to ask you politely to go to the garage, where you're going to commit suicide." Jarvis knocked his cup over and was mopping up the mess as Hawkins continued. "Lauren is there with a body she…you don't want to know where she got it. But you're going to go out there and then we'll work from there. It's the only way that no one will look for you. At least for now. When the shit hits the fan, and it will, she wants you safe. And dead is about as safe as we can make you."

"You could have started with that, that it was a plan and not my actual death." Hawkins laughed a little. "And then what, young man? Am I going to be in hiding for the rest of my life? Or is there more to this plan that I should know."

"Yes, sir, you're going to be living with my parents for a little while, then with a vampire friend of ours, before we ship you off to stay with Lauren. If it comes to that. But when we're done, you'll need to assume the duties of the presidency. We think you're going to do a much better job. But we're putting you in Lauren's home last because of the breach she had this morning. We don't want you to get hurt." Jarvis cleaned up his mess and asked if there was going to be a note. "No. You're just going to do it. Or so they think. We're hoping that this will make them reckless enough to make a big enough mistake so that they hang themselves. And soon too."

Jarvis knew of this man and Lauren, but not only from what he'd been told about them by Joe. Joe had claimed that Lauren had been sleeping her way to her position, and that once there, had decided that she was going to be a glory hound. Jarvis had never actually talked to her, but from everything he'd been able to find about her on his own, she was a more behind the scenes sort of soldier, giving credit to her men more than she took for herself.

Hawkins, too, had been a man that Joe had disliked. But unlike the woman, Jarvis had spoken to him on the night that they had been to the White House and things there had gone terribly wrong. He looked at Hawkins as he was ready to go out of doors, and moved back to his tea pot and unplugged it before speaking, his back to the man and hopefully the camera. Jarvis closed his eyes before asking what he'd been thinking about for some time.

"He tried to have his wife and son killed, didn't he? Joe, I mean. He hired those people to come in and kill his family. It wasn't about him at all. It was his lovely wife and son that were the targets that night." Hawkins said that they'd only recently found out themselves. "He blames you two for them being alive. You messed up whatever plans he had, and now he thinks of it as your fault. Doesn't he?"

"Yes, sir." Jarvis nodded once. It was enough to get him going and do what he needed to stay alive.

Jarvis had heard about his good friend Tony being killed, and he had a feeling it was just a matter of time before he joined him. So far all they'd been able to tell him when he'd asked was that he'd been the victim of a random act of crime. He no more believed that than he did Joe being a good man. As he made his way out to the garage, he stopped long enough to tilt his head up to the softly falling rain and let it wash some of the nightmarish quality of the night and day off him. Jarvis went into the garage with a heavy heart. He didn't want to die. No, he wasn't going to die, at least not tonight, but his feelings on what was going on around him, about him, were sad. Hurtful too.

"Hello, Jarhead. How's it hanging?" Jarvis felt the big arms of Tony wrap around him tightly even as the door behind him closed. "Christ, this had been a shit storm. I'm so glad you're okay with this. It was sort of a spur of the moment kind of thing."

"The paper said you were dead. That your body was missing." Tony looked fit as a fiddle to him. "You're all right. You need to tell...ah, so Lauren has you safely stashed away as well, does she? I'm going to have to thank her in ways that she won't like. That woman...she—"

"No. I was murdered last night. Well, nearly so. My mate found me and brought me back." Jarvis knew that his friend was a tiger and had always thought it funny that he was Tony the Tiger. But the joke, like the Jarhead one, was just between the two of them. "I'm partly vampire and all cat now."

"Partly?" Tony explained. "So you can be out during the day and eat if you want. How the hell did...Christ, did he have you killed too?"

"I'm still trying to figure it out, but I would say yes." Jarvis looked at the beautiful woman that was dressed in black clothing as she moved toward him. "Mr. Vice President, I'm Major Lauren Burcher. I'm glad that we can keep you from harm. But we have to get this going. There are people I need to knock the shit out of as soon as possible."

"So am I, Major, so am I. What do I do now? I've no one left to mourn me overly much. Do you need me to, I don't know, go somewhere right this minute?" She told him that Victoria was going to take him away as soon as he started the car up. "Good. Prints and all. And no note?"

"No. I want people to think on this a little. Like, did you commit suicide or were you killed? Tony being dead will make people wonder, and that's just what we want. Then tomorrow, when it is apparent that you're dead, I'm going to sprinkle a few things around; you know, spice up your life. And so you know, a great many people will mourn your passing."

He wasn't so sure. When he was asked to go ahead and start the car up, he reached in over the body. It took him two tries to get it started. The man in the seat could have been his double.

"We had to make it look good." He nodded at Lauren. "Sir, I swear to you, I didn't kill him because he looked like you."

"Good heavens, I know that." He did too, he realized. "It's just that, well, he could be my twin."

"Dental records will say that it's you. Blood too. We've gone to a great deal of trouble to kill you off to keep you safe." He looked around the garage and asked her where the men where that were supposed to be protecting him. "Gone. And have been for several days. That's why we moved tonight. I was afraid that they were going to make their move sooner than we wanted them to."

As he was wrapped up in the arms of the beautiful woman who said she was taking him to the McCullough's home, he looked at Lauren again as she and Tony set up the car to look like he'd really killed himself. It occurred to him as he was standing in the kitchen of someone else that they knew just what they were doing. And that scared him more than he could say.

~~~

Joe was giddy. Not only that, but he was pretty sure that he could pull out his cock and come, he was so happy. As he made his way to his offices, he tried to hide the smile that had been there since he'd heard not an hour ago that Jarvis was dead.

"You worked fast." He looked at Garth and asked him what he meant. "Taking care of our problem. I thought you were going to wait until the other problem was solved first. The one with the fucking cunt. Did you hear that she shot up those two that we had go to her house? What the fuck do we have to do to get her off our books? Do the job ourselves? I'm tempted, let me tell you."

Joe didn't comment on Garth's threat to do this on his own. The man had done nothing physically at all since he'd been made major general a few years ago, other than get bigger and bigger. He wondered how the man even found clothing to fit him. His uniforms now were straining badly across his belly and arms.

"I really thought you had someone do this." Garth shook his head. "You mean he actually did this on his own? Damn, it's about time he did something to further my career. Did you hear if he left a note or not? That would be fucking fantastic if he did. Saying how he just couldn't live with himself anymore."

"No, not that I've heard, but the secret service is keeping things low key for now. You do know that this fucks up a lot of our shit we have in the works, don't you? I mean, we were going to blame him for their deaths. And then have him kill himself when he realized what a horrific thing he'd done. This makes things easier somewhat, but really does fuck up other plans." Joe didn't want to let go of his happiness for the reality of the situation, and wanted to hit Garth when he brought this up right now. "Who we gonna say killed off the other two now?"

"I'm going to have to look into that, I guess." Joe had two ideas, but neither of them were as good as Jarvis simply going nuts and killing both McCullough and Burcher when they came to be honored in two weeks. It had been a weak plan, but to be honest, they were running out of plans. Nothing he did about Burcher was going right.

"I'm telling you, that bitch has someone telling her that we're moving on her. Every time we think we got her, something happens. And not to mention what it cost us to have those two go in there and get themselves shot to shit. That one had better not talk; not that he'd know all that much, but damn it." Joe said he'd have the man taken care of. "Damned woman must walk around with a fucking gun in her hand all the fucking time. And weren't we told that she was hurt or something? Too sick or injured to even come and see me when I requested it. Maybe she's on to us."

Garth's words had Joe pausing in mid step. Christ, if she even had a hint of what they'd been doing, he didn't want to think about what she'd do to them. Because he'd read enough about her to know that she was an expert at killing, and could ferret out a lie better than any machine that had ever been invented. "Something to think about. She does seem to have a sixth sense about everything we're about to do. I hope to fuck not, but you just don't know about her."

"No, it's not anything I want to think about. I don't want to think about her at all other than to figure out how to tell the world that she's finally fucking dead," Garth said as he followed Joe out of the office.

Joe looked around, and two things occurred to him at once. They were talking about what their plans were in the hallway, and there wasn't a single person around. The latter of the two scared him a great deal. No one was around to hear them, yes, but there was no one there to protect him either.

Usually there were more people roaming these halls than he'd seen in years. Today there wasn't a serviceman meeting him at the door, no secretary running up behind him with a list of shit he was supposed to get done today, and not one secret service agent was where they could see them. He asked Garth what he'd done.

"Done? I don't think I like your tone. What are you talking about?" Joe told him what he was seeing. Garth looked around too, as if he'd not noticed anything amiss either. "Where the hell are they?"

His voice, like that of Joe, was low, a barely audible whisper that had them standing closer to each other to hear. He knew that Garth still carried a weapon, or at least he used to, and wished now that he had one as well. Joe had no idea what was going on, but it frightened him more than a little to see what he was looking at now. Then the movement in front of him had him grabbing for Garth and making a sort of whimpering sound.

"Did you see that?" He nodded at Garth and asked him what it had been. "I'm not sure. But whatever it was, I don't think it's supposed to be here. Fuck man, did you see how fast it moved?"

"Yes." As one, they started down the hall again in the direction the thing had moved. "It looked like a jaguar, don't you think? Or some other kind of cat? Do you think it killed everyone and was just waiting for more food to come its way? Christ, that was the biggest thing I've ever seen, even at the zoo."

"Well, that's a cheery thought. Why would you think it killed everyone off? Do you even see a drop of blood anywhere? If it ate anyone, the halls would be red with it." Joe moved to the door and reached for the handle at the same time that Garth did. His hand was shaking just as badly as his was, he was glad to note, and Joe asked him if he had a gun. "Yes, but believe it or not, it's in my other pants. The ones I wish I was at home wearing right at this moment. In my house and not here with you exposed like this."

The door finally gave and they hurried through the opening to find that it was just like the hallway they'd just left. No one. The desks, all four of them, were empty; even the computer screens were black. No phones were ringing, and there was no one there even to answer them should they start. Moving down the hall to his office, he nearly screamed when Garth bumped into him.

"Damn it, man, are you trying to give me a stroke?" Garth said that he'd seen the cat again. "Where? Where is it?"

"It was just there. By the picture. I swear to you, it's the biggest fucking jag I've ever seen. And trust me, when I go on those hunts I see some pretty big game." Joe nodded. He knew that if Garth said he saw something, he saw it. "We have to get to your office. Now, Joe. It'll be safe there; someone has to be there to keep us safe. That's their fucking jobs. I think we should…hell man, I'm not sure what to think other than I'm scared to death."

But the moment that they entered his office, Joe knew that he was in big trouble. There were no men there in dark suits that would be armed. There was no one that he could command to kill, and there was certainly no one in there that would keep them safe. When Garth plowed into him from the back, he nodded toward the woman sitting in a chair. It was their worst nightmare coming to get them. And Joe had a feeling that life as he knew it before was gone. He was going to jail, if not worse.

"Hello, guys. Have a seat." When neither of them moved, Lauren pulled out her weapon so that they could see it and waved it in the general direction of the chairs. "I didn't ask you to sit. I said to have one. And I'm in no mood to fuck with either of you right now. It's been a really shitty day, in the event you care. Which you should, by the way, but we'll get to that."

"I'll have you court-martialed for this. What the hell do you think you're doing in here? This is my private office. Get out."

Her laughter made his skin crawl, and his temper, a little on the short side, flared up. But he only had to take a single step toward her to see that not only was she armed, but she wasn't alone either. The cat was now standing right next to her with his fur standing on end and his huge teeth showing.

"Now, as I was saying, have a seat. Both of you." Joe moved to his desk, thinking of the gun he had there, and she laughed at him. "Everything that you think you have here has been removed. No guns, no knives. Nothing. Besides, you don't want me to kill you now before the fun begins, do you? Besides, I'm pretty sure that when I'm done here, you'll beg me to take care of you. You two have been pretty busy, haven't you?"

"I don't know what you're talking about. I had a meeting in here this morning and here you are. So if you don't mind, Joe, I'll talk to you later." Before Garth could take a second step to the door, the big cat was on him. Joe watched in horror as the big cat effortlessly knocked the huge man back and sat on his chest. Joe could only think what he'd do to him should he try anything stupid. Then Garth begged. "Please don't kill me. I don't want to die."

Joe knew she was in charge now, but as soon as he was free, which he hoped was soon, he was going to make her pay. He'd had enough of her shit. It was time to cut his losses with her and have her killed. And there would be no mistakes this time either. Garth was freed a few minutes later, and he stood up after wallowing on the floor for ten minutes.

"Have a seat, Garth. You'll be wanting to hear what I have to say as well." Joe sat behind his desk, and just to be sure, he opened his drawer. Not only were his gun and knives gone, but so was his paperwork and pens. He asked her where his things were. "The Feds are going over everything that was in this office. They were able to get into your safes. Both the one in the wall and the one in the floor you had put in. When you have something done, you really should do it yourself, dumbass. There are fewer trails for us to follow. And your home as well, Garth. They seemed to have been informed of a great deal of underhanded work that the two of you are into, and now they have all the proof they need. Shame that your poor wife and son had to find out what a slime ball you are, Joe. She's most helpful now that she's been…enlightened…on a few details of the day Hawkins and I came here."

"What the fuck are you talking about?" But Joe knew as surely as he was sitting there that this woman, this pain in his ass, had ferreted out a great deal of information that he'd thought was well hidden and buried. He had underestimated her one too many times, it seemed. "This is not going to go well for you, Burcher. You wait and see if it doesn't."

Joe picked up the phone to call in security. He wasn't sure who she'd talked to, but he thought if he could get her out of his way for even an hour, he could get the hell out of there. But the moment he picked up the phone, the large cat that had been sitting quietly by Burcher's side leapt up on his desk and put his head to his.

Joe hated cats. Not just the one in front of him but all felines. They acted superior to humans, did what they wanted when they wanted, and it never seemed a human ever came near them. They rarely if ever acknowledged that humans even existed. But this one, he knew without a doubt, would take great joy in killing him right now.

"He's not happy with you either, Joe. I'd put the phone down if I were you. Not that it'll work anyway. I've had that taken care of too. I think, and this is just me, that whoever you're going to call to come rescue you might just put a bullet in your head before I get the chance to. And that would suck, after all the trouble I've gone to, don't you think?" The cat didn't move when he put the phone back. But he did lie down on the desk and stare at him. Joe actually had to cup his cock. He was that fearful of wetting himself.

"I have no idea what you think you're doing, young lady, but whatever your beef is with Joe here, it has nothing to do with me. I'm leaving this place." Joe watched Garth stand again and make his way to the door. As soon as he opened it, Joe knew that he was going to get away, and that just wasn't going to happen. But the moment that he walked out of the opening, he was being backed into the room again by five armed men. The men, all wearing vests, helmets, and armed like there was going to be civil war within the next ten seconds, surrounded the room as Garth was told to sit. Joe would bet anything that they would shoot first, and not give one fuck as to who they were shooting when they did.

"Now. We're going to have a nice long conversation on the things the two of you have been up to. You should know that everything you say is being recorded and has been since you left the residence an hour ago. I believe the phones there have been tapped for a while now, but I don't know that for sure."

Joe looked at Burcher and wanted to get up and strangle her. But there was no way he'd make it any closer than to stand up before the cat in front of him tore his throat out.

"Why are you doing this to us? What the hell have we done to you?" Burcher only stared at him. "All right, we did try to have you killed, but you can't hold that against us when you lived every fucking time. As for anything else that's happened, I'm sure you and I can come to some kind of understanding on that as well. Lauren, this is not the way you treat the president of the United States."

"Really? Then I'd like you to bring back the people that you had killed in the name of your presidency. Because I'm pretty sure that the parents, loved ones, children, and spouses of those that were with me and died would like to have that happen too. Then I'd like nothing better than for you to stand before them, every fucking one of them, and tell them why you did this. Why you felt the need to have your wife and son killed that day. And when that didn't happen because I was doing my job, I want you to explain to them how you wanted revenge and decided that the body count didn't fucking matter to you." Joe said nothing. What would be the point? "According to my count, and I'm pretty sure that I might have missed a few, in your need to see myself and Hawkins dead, you managed to kill over seventy people."

"Most of those killed weren't even Americans." As soon as the words left his mouth, he remembered he was being recorded. "And what kind of information do you think you have about this? None. This is all speculation on your part. You have nothing on me."

The file was dropped on his lap by someone behind him. Joe hated that he flinched, but when he turned and looked at the man coming around the desk, he felt a new kind of fear. Hawkins was a big man, scary too, but right now he looked deadly. Murderous. And he wasn't dressed like the other men, nor did he appear to have a weapon. He thought the man dressed in a polo shirt and jeans was ten times scarier than the men with the weapons. Joe picked up the file with trembling fingers when he was told to open it.

Looking at the information in front of him, he only had to scan the first page to know he was so fucked. And so was Garth. Laying the file on the desk, he looked at Burcher. It was over.

"I want a lawyer."

Chapter 11

Lauren heard the door open and close behind her, but she didn't move off the deck chair. It had been a long last few days and she just wanted it to be quiet. It wasn't as if she didn't want to talk to anyone. She just wasn't in the mood for anyone else telling her that she and Hawkins were heroes. Neither of them, it seemed, felt that way. In a way, she felt sort of dirty.

"That was my mom. She wants to know if you and I would like to come over for dinner tonight. I told her that I'd get back with her." Lauren nodded at Colin. "Can I do anything for you? By the way, I've taken the phone off the hook and told our new staff that we don't want to be disturbed short of the house burning down."

"Good. And no. Even if I knew where to start in getting help, I have no idea what sort it would be. There are so many thoughts going through my head right now, it feels like a washing machine. Things are getting tumbled around too much for me to think about any one thing right now." He sat down and pulled her onto his lap. "I'm sorry."

"Don't be. You've done a lot the last few days, and no one appreciates that as much as I do. My family is safe, you're safe, and we're not hurt or dead. To me, that's a good day." She leaned into his neck and inhaled deeply. "Lauren, talk to me. I want to help you somehow."

Looking out over the woods, she knew the exact spot where the house had been that she'd been a child in. She'd not grown up there—her parents had seen to that—but she had been there. She thought about them.

"My biological parents were nothing like yours. I mean, other than the cat thing, they were human, but they were cruel not just to me but to each other as well. And daily I would wonder if they were going to kill each other or even me. At times I almost wished for it." He didn't tell her he was glad that she'd not done it, whatever it might have taken for her to end her life then, but held her in his arms. It was better than any words he could have said to her. "The week before I escaped, I had been hurt at school. Nothing major, just...well, to be honest with you, I was too weak to fight off any kind of infection and I had cut my leg somewhere. More than likely at the house, and it had grown septic. My parents came to get me, still dressed in their nightclothes, and demanded that I be put back in class. That no matter what, they didn't want me at home and couldn't afford a doctor anyway. Then my father asked them, right then, if there was going to be any compensation for them driving in there on a fool's errand. I knew then that I had to get away from them or die."

"I talked to Peter the other day about you and your parents. He said that he was there before it burned to the ground. He'd gone there to see if anyone else was around, in the event that they might have needed saving. Peter said he was shocked by the living conditions that you were subjected to. That no one, human or not, should have been living there the way things were." Lauren just nodded. She knew that Peter had burned the house down around them. She'd figured that out a few weeks after she'd been living with them. He'd literally saved her by destroying what she'd left behind. "What happened, baby? What was set in motion to get you out of there?"

"The school nurse wasn't a very good one. She wasn't even a nice person, to be honest. Every time I was sent to her office, she would pull on these gloves and not even touch me with them on. She said that I should bathe once a day, and that it was my own fault that I was so dirty that other kids wouldn't play with me." Lauren laughed. "What she didn't know, or didn't care to find out, was that there was only running water in the house when the creek wasn't too low, that even flushing the commode was a chore in that gallons of water had to be brought in to do it. And the few times that we had hot water, it was because the sun had baked the hose that ran from the well and into the house. Otherwise, it was as cold as mountain water could be. But that day, she told my parents that they didn't deserve to have me as their child, or any child. And my father told her she was right, that if she wanted me, then I was all hers. She gagged at the thought."

"She needed to be horsewhipped." Lauren smiled. She'd heard Rich say that on occasion when he was upset about something. "Is she still in the system? Because if she is, then I'd really like to have a few words with her myself."

"I don't know. I would imagine that she is. Even then she was considered ahead of her time in that she thought all kids should have their eyes examined, as well as fluoride treatments. Neither of which I participated in. My parents didn't sign the paperwork." She thought about his original question. "Why I left then.... I guess you could say that terror prompted me into leaving. My parents had been fighting, nothing unusual about that, but this time I was in my room, reading a book. I was nearly out of light when I heard the first gunshot. Then the second one cut the candle I was using in half; it was that close to me. The third one creased my cheek."

"Christ." Colin tightened his hold on her, and she felt loved by it. "And there was no one to help you, was there? No one to come and take you from them?"

"No, no one. I suppose there were grandparents at one time. I'm not even sure who they might be. I know that at one point they were receiving money from one of them, but that cut off when my biological father got arrested for shoplifting. He always said that there was no reason for him not to steal it if they were going to leave it unattended." Her parents would dumpster dive as well as steal. And she knew that at different times in her younger life, both of them had spent time in jail. A few times she'd been left on her own when they were both arrested. "Colin, I need to talk to you about my career. I need...I would like to go back and finish my time there."

"I understand that." She thought there was more to his answer and asked him. "No, there is no 'but.' I really do understand. And according to Tony, you are very close to retiring, and that will be good for you as well."

"They want me to take a desk job. I've thought about it and I might. It would be nice to be home nightly and have weekends off with you." He laughed a little. "What was that about?"

"You made it sound like we'd not be spending any time through the week together. And I have news for you; we'll be spending a lot of time together." She said nothing, wondering what the hell she was going to be doing with herself once her service was up. "I'd like to talk to you about children."

"I don't know anything about them. Other than Pete, I've never spent a great deal of time with them." Her body stiffened at the thought of being around children, and she was pretty sure he knew how scared she was of it. "Perhaps we can ease into that for now."

"There is a couple that I know that are having twins. And they're getting a divorce. It's not a nice, easy one. A nasty one, they're both saying, and the children would be tossed back and forth between the two of them and at times, and because I know them both, the kids would be pawns in their plan to hurt the other. The woman is putting them up for adoption, and the father is okay with that. I think this is the best decision that the two of them have ever made." She sat up on his lap and looked at Colin. "She's only about three months along and willing to sign them over to us the moment they're born."

"You already talked to her about it?" Colin told her he had not, but that Gab, his friend, had talked to him about who he knew that would take them and care for them. "But they don't know that you want to take them?"

"No. And it wouldn't be just me. It would be us both raising any children we might have or adopt. And if you're not ready for that, that's just fine with me as well. I know of a couple of other people that they can talk to. And since I know that the children will be safe with either of them, I'm okay with telling them we're not interested at this time." She leaned back on his chest and asked him why he thought they could make this work, having children in the house. "I'm out of work right now and could easily be a full-time father while you finished up your time. Larson has taken over all the projects I was working on, and is loving the freedom of making his own choices and decisions. We have enough money and resources that it wouldn't be financially straining on us. I'm not...well, since meeting you, I'm not insecure with the knowledge that women, most of them as a matter of fact, can do a job better than me. And do more."

"But babies. You know anything about them? I don't." He said that he had the greatest resource around: his mom and dad. "Yeah, she and your dad did a great job on raising you guys. Even with what they had to work with."

He tickled her, and she laughed with him. As they settled again, she thought about children, these kids, and what bringing them into their life might mean. Being a parent was a big deal. She thought maybe she might rather face a firing squad than try and figure out a kid's wants and needs.

"They'd know that we're not their real parents. As soon as they're old enough to know. I'm assuming that they're not cats, right?" He said they were humans, so they would know. "I'm not saying yes to this, but what would your family think? I mean, first of all, they won't be cats, as you said, and I didn't have them for you."

"I doubt very much my parents would care if we picked them out of the garden so long as they could babysit a lot. My brothers would be thrilled to know that there are babies in the house. And if they're girls, we'd have built-in protectors when they dated. If we let them date. Also, as their mom, I'm sure you'd be teaching them the best ways to protect themselves and how to hurt a man when they don't think no means no." She would teach them how to protect themselves in all situations, not just dating. "If you don't want to adopt them, we can wait and have some of our own."

"Adopting sounds good. I mean, I'd really like to have children too. Just not yet. I only have four and a half years to go to get my twenty-five. Then I can retire with a lot better package." He didn't mention, and neither did she, that she was able to have that all now because of what she'd done recently. "And then there is the matter of trial for Wilson and Irvin too."

They were both in prison, along with nine other men that had been mentioned in the information that they'd gotten from the offices of the two men. Joe had had a separate home that he worked and played in, one that not even his wife knew about. Everyone was still trying to figure out how he'd gotten in and out of the residence without anyone knowing. Lauren was sure that more names were going to be added to the list of people involved in this.

Butch Daily, the cohort of the two men, was facing more charges as he'd been found with an arsenal of weapons and other weapons of mass destruction in his home when they'd caught up with him. He was in federal prison awaiting other charges that came up when his prints were put into the system. His list of aliases was as long as his rap sheet. Butch had also been there when she and Hawkins had been shot, and had thought, like the rest of the world, that she and Hawkins would never make it back to the States alive.

"I love you, Lauren." She looked at him and realized that as much as he loved her, she did him even more. "Whatever you want to do, wherever you need to be, I'm here for you. You are my world."

The two of them sat there for a little while longer. The phone in the house rang a couple of times. Colin's cell phone vibrated in his pocket too. Neither of them, it seemed, wanted anything to do with the outside world at the moment. Then Colin laughed and sat her up a little.

"My brother Dustin is on his way over. He has a project he wants to talk to you about." She asked him what it was. "He and Dad renovated this building downtown, and they want to turn it into an after school place for older kids. He wants to talk to you about it."

"If he wants me to paint or something like that, I'm his man, but I know shit about after school stuff." Colin laughed and said that wasn't it. "Then what possible reason can he have for asking me for help?"

"Most of the kids are bullied. Some of them are the bullies. He wants to bring you in so that you can teach them the right way to protect themselves, and to put the others on the right path. I think it's called it a scared shitless approach. He said that a few of the kids could use some outlet for their pain. As in their parents are hurting them and they need to learn to keep themselves safe from them." She knew that pain, and stood up to go to the railing. "He seems to think that you might know a few people, retired servicemen, who can come in and give a hand too. Mentoring program, so to speak."

"You mean have a bunch of foul mouthed men who served their country come in and talk to a bunch of teenagers about what they're going through? I think most of them would rather go back overseas and fight again." She knew that she would. "I'll ask, but don't expect any big deal made out of it."

Colin stood up then too and came to stand beside her. He was forever touching her, running his hand down her arm to her hand, hugging her before moving on. It was comforting and loving, two things she would never have thought of herself looking forward to.

When the doorbell rang, Colin went in to answer it. Almost as soon as he was gone, Victoria appeared. She wasn't really there—it was the brightest part of the day— but she did look like she was. Lauren asked after Tony and saw the change in her friend's face immediately.

"He's well. And feisty. He has big plans now that we're together. I think he is retiring as well from the service." Lauren didn't mention what she and Colin had talked about, but told her that she was happy for them both. "I have come to ask a favor of you. It's not a big one, but one that only you can help me with."

"Anything, you know that. I owe you more than I could ever repay." Victoria said the same was thought of her. "I'm just so glad that we met all those years ago. Our lives might have turned out differently had we not."

"Yes. I would be dead." Lauren started to tell her she was sorry about that again, but she waved her off. "What I need is for you to help me with a home. The one that I have...well, it served its purpose when it was only me. And now I find that I wish for something homey. The place I have now is not even fit for a vampire, much less one with a mate."

"I'm guessing that you don't want to live in Tony's home." She said that he did not, that he wanted a home with her, not memories from before. "All right. I know that Rich and Dustin have a couple of homes that they're working on now. Maybe you can talk to them and they can make any adjustments you need in a home now while it's still under construction."

"I would like that. And a bigger home as well. I should like to have you and the rest of the jamboree to come and visit us." Lauren said that would be nice. "There is one more thing too."

Victoria seemed a little hesitant about saying anything, so Lauren thought of something to fill the time until she was ready. She told her of the babies that they may or may not adopt and the plans that Dustin wanted her to help out with. Lauren was pretty sure she hadn't been listening to her, and wasn't really surprised when Victoria turned to her suddenly, her face awash with guilt.

"You will not find the men who shot Tony. Their bodies will be…when I took them away that day, I told no one that they lived. Not even Tony." It was abrupt and to the point, and Lauren didn't even ask her why not. "If you could tell someone where the bodies are…they are not in the best of shape to identify, but I have left their things there so that they can be…dental records will do very little to help them, I think. I was…as you say, pissed when I went back to them."

"I see." She didn't and was sure she didn't want to either. "Tell me where they are and I can tell a couple of people I know that are working on the case. No one will know where the information came from. I think that having something like this solved, even this way, will be one less thing that the authorities have to fuck with right now."

"Thank you." There was more, Lauren knew it, but again spoke of things that weren't related to the trouble Victoria seemed to be having. She told her of her interview, or whatever it was going to be, with Jarvis who, of course, was now the president.

"I think he'll do a good job. He's still working from his home, of course. They have to make sure that his new digs are not going to blow or anything. I suppose that we should be happy that—"

"I want to kill them." Just because she wanted to be sure they were on the same page, she asked her who. "Irwin and Wilson. They ordered Tony to be killed, and now they're sitting in their cells living their life like nothing has changed."

They were. But their lives had changed a great deal. The two of them were in protective custody right now, but as soon as the trial was over, Lauren didn't think they'd last long in prison. Even not being in the general population, they'd still be killed quickly, and not quietly either.

"If you kill them, and I'm not saying they don't deserve it, what would that give you? You have Tony now and he's well. And will be for a good long time too. They're going to pay for what they did. More than likely with their deaths. But not right away." Victoria nodded. "Killing them would be a great deal of satisfaction to a lot of people, but they also need to stand up for what they've done. They killed a great many people in the name of greed. All those young men that were there to kill Hawkins and my company just so they could be in charge of everything."

"I know. I knew that you'd say that too. It's why I came to you instead of following through on what I want to do. You level me at times, I hope you know that." Lauren told her that she did the same for her.

Colin and Dustin came in then. They both looked like they'd been laughing. And when Colin asked about Tony, Victoria smiled. "He is having a grand time whipping his men into shape. He said that they've been lax much too long with him being away. I think I like him being in charge. It's…invigorating to me."

Colin laughed and Dustin's face turned several shades of red. Lauren just giggled. Victoria, Lauren knew, was around more people than she had been in years. And her *just say it* attitude was something people were going to have to get used to about her. She was much too old to change.

~~~

Colin moved slowly between the trees. He wanted to catch Lauren unawares again, but it was getting harder and harder to do so. She had caught on quickly on how to sneak as a cat, and her knowledge as a soldier was making it difficult for him to tackle her the way he wanted to. He loved to pounce.

There are nine deer on the property right now, and a wolf that I've never seen. How do you tell if they're shifter or not? He told her it was their smell. And it surprised him that he wasn't worried about her being there with someone she didn't know. *Ah, so I have to get up close and personal with his ass, or is it just a general smell to them?*

There will be no ass smelling unless you're near mine, and even then, I'm not so sure. So yes, it's just a general smell. You should be able to smell human on them. More so than a regular wolf unless he's been raised by them. I'm doubting that, but you never know with people. She didn't say anything back, and he got a little worried. *Where are you?*

You mean the big bad Colin McCullough can't find his little mate? Oh, how sad is that. He growled at her, then saw the deer she'd been talking about. *You should be able to see me in the thicket behind the big buck. He looks like he could take on a few hundred wolfs as big as he is.*

I see you. Anyone could, as a matter of fact, once she was out in the open. She was snowy white with darker spots that stood out in deep contrast to her fur. He was a darker orange with the same darker spots, and was what he thought of as a run of the mill jag. But her coloring was more suited to desert running, and he loved it. He saw the wolf then. *He's not a shifter. Too small. I forgot to mention that too. Unless he's a pup, which I doubt. Just watch him. He looks...well, he looks like he's going to take one of the deer.*

Will he attack the group or just take what he needs? Colin said he didn't know. That if he was hungry enough he might, but they would normally stand down with so many. *He does look a little on the thin side. What if we helped him out? You know, put out food for him. Maybe he'll leave the deer around here alone.*

All right. He started to ask her why she cared, but then he saw the two pups coming out of the tree line. That was the reason, he realized, that the big wolf was taking a chance with the group of deer. He had young to feed. *Lauren, head the pups off a little and I'll help the wolf get his dinner. They're starving. Look how small the pups are. I wonder how long they've been out here like this.*

I don't know, but I'm worried now. You mean to kill the deer, don't you? He didn't answer her. *I guess it's the way of the wild, but I don't have to like it. I know all about food chain and all, but why would he wait so long to get food when they're this starved?*

I don't know, love. Maybe he's been on the run for a long time, or he's just arrived and this is the first time he's been able to find meat. But they have to eat. He watched her move to the pups, and the wolf was slightly distracted.

Colin went in for the kill and was surprised when the wolf came to help him. The two of them took the larger of the females down, and then Colin backed away. He'd done this before, killed wild animals that were harming other wild life, but never had he done it for food. He watched the wolf, seeing that he really was nearly starved as he tore open the flesh of the deer and then looked at him. Backing away more, Colin wanted him to know that he wasn't going to harm any of them.

The two cubs came up behind their father and dove into the fresh meat as if they'd been waiting for some sort of signal to do so. Now that they were closer, he could see that they were all in the same shape. Nodding to the wolf and leaving him to his dinner, he moved to stand beside Lauren. Then they made their way to the house.

He would have died, I think, had we not helped him. Colin said nothing, not even sure what he might have said. The wolves, like a lot of other animals, were hunted for sport now, and he was worried that they might hunt them out. *I want to set up some sort of rescue park around here. For him and other wolves. Or for that matter, whatever animal needs a little help.*

They're wild. I'm not saying that I don't like your idea, but they're wild animals and could hurt us. She said then they'd take care of them. *All right. I'm not sure what we'd have to do, but we can look into it.*

When they were on the deck, both of them shifted and then moved to the large hot tub that had only just arrived today. He had never been a big fan of them. It seemed that they would never relax him the way people said they did. But with Lauren, it was nice; the warmed water and jets seemed to make his muscles, usually so sore from working too much, just feel good. As soon as they were both in the water, the jets were turned on and he nearly melted. It felt that wonderful.

"Dustin gave me a schedule to help out with the club of sorts. I still can't believe he talked me into this." Colin didn't say anything. He had been surprised as well, but then once she said yes, she threw herself into it like most things she did. "And tomorrow I go in and talk to Jarvis. He said he wants me to head up some kind of death squad. I told him not to expect too much from me. I have a life now."

"Death squad?" She told him it was a hunt and destroy kind of thing to go in and retrieve people from behind enemy lines. "Will Hawkins be with you?"

"No." He knew when she was stalling and waited her out. "He's going to go into something else. Something that I can't share with you. But I won't be going on the missions, just making sure from here that the men know where to go and when."

"And how do you feel about not being right there where the action is?" She leaned back in the seat and closed her eyes. He loved her, everything about her, and seeing her this way, relaxed and happy, made his heart beat a little easier. "I know you're going to have to visit DC a few times a month. Tony told me that a few days ago."

"Yeah, he told me too. It's something we have to talk about." He nodded and wondered if she'd be upset if he asked her if he could go with her. "Tony and I have talked about the visits there. I guess he's going to be setting us up a house to stay in so we don't have to hotel it and everything. There will be a staff too. He seems to think it would be easier on us if we didn't have to have our stuff shifted around every time we came to town."

"That's good." It was too. He wasn't going to have to be without her at night. "Oh, Mom said to tell you that she's conducting interviews for you over the next few days for staff here. I had no idea that it was that much work. We do have the few that came with me, but she thinks that with us working both here and out of state, we might need some extra help."

"Neither did I, but she's right about us working a great deal. And to be honest, the thought of having strangers in the house all the time is a little overwhelming. I know that we will both be out a lot, but do we need a cook all the time? And someone to make our beds?" He looked at her. "And if anyone tries to dress or undress me besides you, then they're going to get their throat punched." Colin laughed and shook his head. The things that came out of her mouth at times were so serious, yet funny as hell.

"I think they're mostly here so we don't have to worry about fixing dinner if we've been out all day. And I, for one, would love to have someone make the bed and dust for us. I hated that when I lived alone, and welcomed someone coming in and doing it for me." He could tell that she was going to sleep. As he moved closer to her, just to keep her from going under the water, she looked at him and he smiled. "I am so in love with you."

"I want those twins." He nodded, stilling in his movements to let her finish. "They'll need us. Not just because they don't need to be in the system, but with them not being wanted...I know how that feels when you're little. If we raise them...when we raise them, we'll make sure that they never feel that way. That no one treats them as if they are less than what they are, and that they can do whatever they want. The sky is the limit."

"All right. I love that idea." She nodded and laid her head back. "They're one of each, by the way. I was told that this morning when I talked to Jack."

"Okay, good to know for the next phase our life. We'll need to add more room on this house." He looked at the house and wondered why she thought that. "We can't just have these two, you know. We'll need to make sure that your parents and mine have plenty of grandchildren to spoil. As I'm sure they'll do."

"I'm sure you're right. The children will fill a big hole in all our lives." He pulled her on his lap and suckled at her breasts when she lifted them to his mouth. "How about we practice making a few of our own while we're here?"

"I love the way your mind works."

Chapter 12

"Josh, we have company." She heard him moving in the cab behind her but didn't turn to make sure he was hidden. They'd been on the run for a long time now, and this was nothing new for either of them. The police would come in, take a look around, then leave her to her business. They were never going to find Josh unless they knew what he was. Only this time they were all dressed in suits, and she was sure that two of them, if not all three, were armed.

The man standing at her door when she rolled down the window asked her what her name was. Reese said nothing. If he didn't know then she wasn't going to help him unless he made her. When he laughed, she watched the other two with him, both cops, as they moved to stand by the other door to her truck.

"Miss Farley, you're only making this harder on yourself. We know that Josh Savage isn't your nephew, and we also know that he's with you. Just tell us where you have him and we'll let you go on your way." Reese said nothing but kept her hands were they could all see them if they were inclined. "Why don't you step out of the rig and we'll talk."

"Am I in trouble?" The man said nothing, and she didn't move. "I'm afraid you'll have to do better than that. I'm not going to move out of here until you tell me what you're talking about."

Two men that she knew from years on the road came out of the diner she'd just been in. They were big burly men, both of them tatted up from head to foot and actually just as kind and cuddly as a kitten. But they were also not ones to be fucked with.

"You all right, honey?" Bone, the man that she'd only just found out his name, came up to lean on her door. He wasn't moving, she thought, and looked at the man behind him. Suit wasn't impressed. "He bothering you?"

"He wants me to get out of my rig, and he thinks I have someone with me. When I asked if I was in some sort of trouble, I didn't get an answer." Bone turned to look at Suit. "The other two are at my passenger door."

"Doug has them." She didn't even look. If Bone said they were with Doug, then she was pretty sure they weren't going to be opening her door any time soon. "And we've called in the law. Don't care much for them myself, but they might have a thing or two to say to these dick heads."

"This has nothing to do with you gentlemen. I would really appreciate it if you left us to our business." Bone only looked up at her with a wink. "Did you hear me?"

"I heard you just fine as a matter of fact. I don't give two shits, but I heard you."

Bone looked down the road, and Reese looked in her mirror to see what he was looking for. Dust was flying up the road, and she'd bet anything that it was the police. She really didn't want to see them either, but right now she thought they might be the lesser of two evils.

"You called the police? What the hell for?" Reese said nothing as Suit took a few steps toward her. That was as far as he got before Bone put his hand out and stopped him. She could see the knife in his hand even if Suit couldn't. "This isn't over, Reese. We're going to get you and that kid. You'd better think on that when you drive out of here with him."

When the man took off running, Reese thought of all the things she had to think of now every time she left someplace. This man's threats would be foremost in her mind, but nothing more than the million and one things she had to worry about now. Josh flew up and sat on the seat next to her. His pretty feathers ruffled with his anger.

The police, of course, arrived just as Suit was peeling out of the drive, leaving his two men behind to be dealt with. They explained to the cops what they knew. The police, local boys all of them, asked to see the inside of her rig for the kidnapped boy.

Reese opened the door a little and Josh, as his bird, flew out of the cab and took to the skies. She felt a little better then, knowing that he was safe for the time being as the police climbed up in her rig and had a look around. If they thought it strange that she was a long haul driver or that she had a big cab for one person, they didn't say anything. As soon as they finished with whatever it was they were doing, she was free to go.

"You see this man again, you make sure you let someone know. I don't know what his issue was with you, but his men were set on detaining you. And they have the weapons to try." Nodding at the cop, she started her truck and let it idle while he continued. "Bone said you come through here a lot, that he's never seen you with anyone but yourself and that bird of yours. Will he come back?"

"He will. When I'm down the road." She didn't tell him that the hawk was watching them and would, if necessary, shift into something larger to save her, but the cop nodded again and she pulled out into the road. It was probably an hour later when Josh flew in the opposite window and shifted to his human self.

"That man, he made a phone call when he got down the road to the hotel. He called his boss and told him you got away again." Reese asked him if he was all right. "I am. Just fine and dandy. But I do think we need to find us a place to lay low for a couple of days. What about you?"

"I'm fine, and yes. I agree." She asked him if he knew of any place that they could hide their home in and be safe too. "You do know that they're going to be looking harder for me now. I know that we've been pulled up before, but they've never had guns out in the open either."

"They're getting desperate, I think." She just glanced at Josh and told him to buckle up. As he did it, he continued with what he'd found out. "They're thinking that if they can get you to come with them, whether easily or not, that I'll come running to save you. I want you to know right now, I wouldn't do that. I don't even like you."

"I don't care all the much for you either." They both laughed, knowing that they had grown closer than family over the last four years. "The next town we come to, I'll see about finding a place for us to pull in and hide out. A nice hotel, even a little one, would be a good change for us. Maybe a place with a kitchenette that I can cook something other than leftovers in."

They drove for a few more miles, Josh not saying anything much, but she knew he was upset. The two of them had been on the run for a long time now, and she was getting sick of it. Not that she'd stop taking care of him, not for any amount of money in the world, but she was tired.

The pull off came up, and while he dozed in his seat, she eased into it. The surrounding forest was thick for this time of year, but she knew as soon as the fall started to drop the cover, they'd have to be on the run again. As soon as the rig stopped, she sat back on the seat and closed her eyes. It had been a long time since either of them had had any kind of rest.

"There was a help wanted sign in that diner we passed." She'd seen it too and asked him if he thought she should apply for it. "It would go a long way in getting us a place to stay, don't you think?"

"Yes. But what about you? I can't stand the thought of you having to be hidden away all the time. It's pretty out and you should be enjoying it." He only cocked a brow at her. "What I mean is, with other children. Not flying above them or running along the ground like a wolf. There are things that kids do that you're missing out on."

"I'm pretty sure that we both know that I'm not much of a social kid." He wasn't, and she wasn't either. That was why they were good for each other. "I'll go ahead of you and find you a place to stay. Once you're in, I'll come to you. Then tomorrow or the next day, you can see about that job."

As they gathered up what she could carry by herself, she thought of working. Her rig was a good source of income for them, when she could find work that was. But lately it had been harder for her. She thought now it was because of the man that had accosted her in the parking lot. He'd put the word out that she wasn't to have work.

It might have sounded like she was paranoid. Really, she supposed that she was. But she was pretty sure that she was right. Things had been getting harder and harder for her and Josh lately, and she was worried that the next time they stopped to get gas in their moving home, there would be no money to fill the tanks. Her resources were running dangerously low.

The walk into town was uneventful. Josh would come back and swoop over her, making her laugh, but for the most part she was alone. An occasional car or truck would go by, but with Josh warning her they were coming, she'd have enough time to hide out until they passed her.

She was just coming into the town proper when she saw the two men. They weren't the men from today. And for some reason she thought that they'd have nothing to do with them either. They looked…well, safe came to mind. A word that she'd not been able to use in the positive way in a long time. As she moved to the other side of the street from them, keeping an eye on their movements, she tried to think what about them had her feeling so weirded out.

They're shifters. Josh could communicate with her, but she couldn't talk back to him. They weren't sure why, but at times like this, it was helpful to her to know what he was thinking. *Not like me, but cats. Jaguars. The older man is the younger man's father.*

No one was like Josh, but she understood what he meant. They weren't able to shift into anything other than what they were now and their cats. Josh could shift into anything. Going into the little hotel, she hoped they'd not be there long, or they'd be living on the streets with her hunk of metal of a home rotting away in the field she'd left it in.

"I was looking for a job too. Nothing fancy. I noticed the diner had a help wanted sign. Do you know anything about it?" The woman behind the counter asked her if she could cook. "I can, as a matter of fact. I love it."

"I'm the owner. I'm looking for someone to come in and do the breakfast for me. Too much work for me anymore. I'd like to just close up, but the town, they love coming in and gabbing while they eat. They said it's not gossiping, but I don't know what it would be other than that. When can you show me what you can do?" Reese told her that she could do it now if she wanted. "That'll be just fine. Just fine indeed. I got to go over soon and start on the dinner stuff. You mind going over and getting it ready? Margaret, my sister, she can show you around and tell you what is what."

Reese was so excited that she nearly gave her real name when she asked her. "Anna. Anna Reese. I'll go over as soon as I get my things in my room. Thank you."

As she made her way to the room, she was nearly giddy with relief. Even if she only worked for a couple of weeks, it would be great to have a stove under her again and to have a nice bed for a change. She told Josh all about it when he came in a few minutes after she did.

Going into the diner twenty minutes later, she was happy to see that the elderly woman was ready for her. She showed her around, then told her that the menu for the night was up to her, that she didn't want to mess with it.

"You go on and see what we got in there and you cook it up. The only standard we have is burgers and fries, plus them winger things." It took her a few seconds to realize she meant wings, a popular thing for the last few years. "And beer. But you don't have to worry none about that. I'll be tending bar tonight until May gets here."

As soon as she entered the kitchen, her domain according to Margaret, she knew that at least for now, she was going to be having some fun. Pulling out the ingredients to start on dinner, Reese realized something else. Josh was going to be eating well too. Margaret had told her that all leftovers were hers to do with what she wanted. She was taking them home with her.

Paranormal Romance with a Bite!
Blood, Body and Mind:
A Paranormal Romance by Kathi S. Barton

Your FREE Copy is Waiting...

Aaron MacManus, the new master vampire of the realm just wanted to go out and meet some of his subjects and to figure out what needed to be done to set things right.

April and Demetrius Carlovetti own an air service and are the most trusted and well liked vampires in Aaron's realm. What he didn't expect when he visited them was betrayal. His own bodyguards try to murder him and blame it on the Carlovetti's.

Sara Temple was not a vampire. She pilots planes for the Carlovetti Airways. She had secretes of her own and working for this small air service is keeping her out of sight. The last thing she wanted to do was save a vampire, even an extremely good looking one.

Sara was only trying to survive but with Aaron she becomes embroiled in politics, the magic of several realms involving a queen in peril, magical beings, passion and love.

Blood, Body and Mind, the first book in the Aaron's Kiss series.

Available on the following devices and systems

Join my Readers' Group and get a copy of Blood, Body and Mind FREE

http://eepurl.com/brCBvP

http://eepurl.com/brCBvP

Before You Go...

HELP AN AUTHOR

write a review

THANK YOU!

Share your voice and help guide other readers to these wonderful books. Even if it's only a line or two your reviews help readers discover the author's books so they can continue creating stories that you'll love. Login to your favorite retailer and leave a review. Thank you.

Kathi Barton, author of the bestselling series Force of Nature, lives in Nashport, Ohio with her husband Paul. In addition to writing full time Kathi likes to spend time with her eight grandkids, three children and three children-in-laws. She writes to relax and have fun.

Her muse, a cross between Jimmy Stewart and Hugh Jackman brings them to life for her readers in a way that has them coming back time and again for more. Her favorite genre is paranormal romance with a great deal of spice. You can visit Kathi on line and drop her an email if you'd like. She loves hearing from her fans. aaronskiss@gmail.com.

Follow Kathi on her blog:
http://kathisbartonauthor.blogspot.com/

www.ingramcontent.com/pod-product-compliance
Lightning Source LLC
Chambersburg PA
CBHW032128170626
46808CB00006B/2150